Dan

the one that
horse and k
and hollerin

Yeah, he knew what Gabriella was playing at. He
was only too happy to play along.

The moment that thought crossed his mind, it
dragged a different thought along for the ride. What
if this—the sob story about her mom, the smiles,
especially the kiss—all of it was just playing? What if
she was playing him?

He'd thought her brother had been one of his best
friends—a man he could trust with his life. Where
had that gotten him?

What if she was just trying to muck up the works
with her bright smiles and warm looks and sweet,
hot kisses? What if she was trying to get him
distracted or off balance?

What if she was using him?

But why? That was the question he couldn't answer.

He wanted to protect her, by God.

But who would protect him from her?

* * *

What a Rancher Wants is a
Texas Cattleman's Club: The Missing Mogul novel—
Love and scandal meet in Royal, Texas!

* * *

If you're on Twitter,
tell us what you think of Harlequin Desire!
#harlequindesire

Dear Reader,

Welcome back to Royal, Texas! Things have been changing for the members of the Texas Cattleman's Club. Alex Santiago has been found, but his old friend Chance McDaniel is still living under a cloud of suspicion that he had something to do with Alex's disappearance.

Chance is mighty tired of the rumors flying around town—including the one where he abducted Alex because Alex stole Cara Windsor from him. Chance just wants his life back—and he wants some answers.

When he hears that Alex's family has come north of the border to Royal, he decides to go talk to them and find out why Alex was operating under a different name. What else was that man lying about?

The answer opens the door. Alex has a sister, Gabriella del Toro. Gabriella is a sheltered young woman who's managed to build a successful jewelry business despite the limits placed upon her by her father. Gabriella longs to be free to do as she wishes, but her father's concerns for her safety make normal things, like riding horses or dating, a challenge.

Until she meets Chance. One look at the cowboy and she's smitten. But can she trust her heart to the man who may have harmed her brother?

What a Rancher Wants is a sensual story about becoming the person you were always meant to be. It was a great honor to be asked to be a part of the Texas Cattleman's Club! I hope you enjoy reading this book as much as I enjoyed writing it! Be sure to stop by www.sarahmanderson.com and join me as I say long live cowboys!

Sarah

WHAT A
RANCHER WANTS

—

SARAH M. ANDERSON

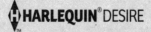

Special thanks and acknowledgment to Sarah M. Anderson
for her contribution to the
Texas Cattleman's Club: The Missing Mogul miniseries.

Recycling programs
for this product may
not exist in your area.

ISBN-13: 978-0-373-73295-1

WHAT A RANCHER WANTS

Printed in U.S.A.

Books by Sarah M. Anderson

Harlequin Desire

  A Man of His Word #2130
  A Man of Privilege #2171
  A Man of Distinction #2184
  A Real Cowboy #2211
*Straddling the Line #2232
*Bringing Home the Bachelor #2254
*Expecting a Bolton Baby #2267
  What a Rancher Wants #2282

*The Bolton Brothers

Other titles by this author available in ebook format.

SARAH M. ANDERSON

Award-winning author Sarah M. Anderson may live east of the Mississippi River, but her heart lies out West on the Great Plains. With a lifelong love of horses and two history teachers for parents, she had plenty of encouragement to learn everything she could about the tribes of the Great Plains.

When she started writing, it wasn't long before her characters found themselves out in South Dakota among the Lakota Sioux. She loves to put people from two different worlds into new situations and to see how their backgrounds and cultures take them someplace they never thought they'd go.

One of Sarah's books, *A Man of Privilege,* won the *RT Book Reviews* 2012 Reviewers' Choice Best Book Awards Series: Harlequin Desire.

When not helping out at her son's school or walking her rescue dogs, Sarah spends her days having conversations with imaginary cowboys and American Indians, all of which is surprisingly well-tolerated by her wonderful husband. Readers can find out more about Sarah's love of cowboys and Indians at www.sarahmanderson.com.

To Amy, who always appreciates a good Texasism—
and a good Texan! The best kinds of friends
are the ones where it doesn't matter how long
it's been or where you are—you're always able
to pick up right where you left off.

One

"*¡Dios mío!*" Gabriella del Toro hissed under her breath. Blood welled up from the cut she'd inflicted upon herself with the can opener. She sighed. As if anything else could have gone wrong.

From his seat at the breakfast table, Joaquin, her bodyguard, looked up from his tablet. "I'm fine," she said, answering his unspoken question. "Just a cut."

She looked down at the injury. She had not anticipated that fixing some broth and toast for her brother, Alejandro, would be so difficult. But then, everything was difficult right now. While she had spent time in the kitchen back at Las Cruces, the ancestral del Toro estate west of Mexico City, she'd never actually prepared anything more than tea and coffee. Their cook had thought that preparing meals was beneath the lady of the house, even if the lady had been only twelve. No one had thought to teach Gabriella the first thing about cooking since...her *tía* had tried to show her how to make tortillas from scratch.

Gabriella had been seven the last time Papa had taken her and Alejandro to see their mother's sister. A full twenty years had passed since then.

As Gabriella rinsed the cut under the faucet and wrapped her wounded finger in a towel, she mentally bemoaned how this must look. She was the daughter of Rodrigo del Toro, one of the most powerful legitimate businessmen in all of Mexico. She was one of the most sought-after jewelry designers in Mexico City. She regularly transformed hunks of metal and pieces of rock into wearable art with a Mayan influence.

But at this moment, she was every heiress stereotype rolled into one. She couldn't even open a can of soup.

The bleeding staunched, she went looking for a bandage. She heard Joaquin stand and trail her out of the kitchen, although he kept a polite distance. She'd rarely been apart from the large, mostly silent man since her father had hired him to protect her when she had been thirteen. She was now twenty-seven. Joaquin Baptiste was nearing forty, but he had showed no signs of slowing down. Secretly, Gabriella hoped he never would. He was far more concerned with her happiness than her father—or even her brother—had ever been. That, and he had never let any harm befall her. Even if it did make dating…challenging.

She walked to the bathroom and found a box of bandages in a cabinet, mentally cursing her clumsiness the whole time. The cut was on the edge of her index finger. It would make holding pliers while she shaped wire almost impossible.

Gabriella caught herself. Her pliers were not here, nor were any of her other jewelry-making supplies. It had not been possible to pack up all her tools. Besides, she had been under the impression that they would only be in America long enough to collect Alejandro.

Her poor brother. Her poor father, for that matter. The del Toro family was forever haunted by the specter of abductions, but they'd all thought Alejandro would be safe in Texas. Kidnappings for profit weren't nearly as common in America as they were in Mexico, Alejandro had argued when Rodrigo had hatched this scheme to send him north to America to "investigate" an energy company he wanted to acquire. Alejandro had refused to bring Carlos, his personal guard. He had told Rodrigo he would not go if he weren't allowed to do things the American way.

The thing that Gabriella still could not believe was that their father had relented and Alejandro had been allowed to live alone, as an American would. Alejandro had assumed the identity of Alex Santiago and come north alone a little more than two years ago.

Gabriella had suffered a bout of jealousy at that. She longed to be free to come and go as she pleased, but her father would not hear of it. She had stayed at Las Cruces, under constant watch of Joaquin—and Rodrigo.

At least, she had been jealous—until Alejandro had been kidnapped. However, the kidnappers had not demanded an exorbitant ransom, as was the usual custom. Instead, there had been no word from them—or Alejandro, until he had been found in the back of a coyote's truck. Coyotes smuggled immigrants. Alejandro, the son of Rodrigo del Toro, had been thrown in with the poor things desperate to start a new life in America.

The kidnappers had not treated Alejandro well. Although his wounds were healing, he had no memory of the attack, which meant he had no information to give the law-enforcement officers who occasionally checked on him. The case had stalled. Alejandro had returned, mostly whole, to his home in Royal, Texas. Now that his life was no longer in immediate danger, Gabriella had gotten the sense that the police weren't as dedicated to finding the criminals who had abducted him in the first place. Still, they were "requesting" that Alejandro remain in the country. Truthfully, Alejandro had showed no signs of wanting to go. He stayed in his room, resting or watching football— what the Americans called soccer.

Alejandro showed almost no signs of memory, except

his love of football. He didn't seem to remember her, or Papa. In fact, the only reaction they'd gotten out of him beyond a mumbled thank-you when she brought him his meals was when Papa had announced they would be returning to Las Cruces within the week. Only then had Alejandro sparked to life, insisting that he was not going anywhere. Then he had locked himself in his room.

So Rodrigo had set up temporary headquarters in a set of rooms in Alejandro's home in Royal that had recently been home to Mia Hughes, the former housekeeper. Papa was simultaneously running Del Toro Energy and utilizing his vast resources to identify the culprits that had taken Alejandro. Rodrigo was not about to let anyone get away with assaulting any member of his family. Gabriella could only hope that, when he caught the perpetrators, he wouldn't do something that would land him in an American prison.

Which meant that Gabriella had no idea how long the del Toro family would be trapped in this house together.

This was also why Joaquin was standing outside the bathroom as Gabriella tended her injury. If she had ever hoped of having the kind of freedom that Alejandro had tasted for two years, those hopes were now dashed. Her father would not allow her to go unguarded. Not after nearly losing his son.

Still, she was in America instead of in Las Cruces, and that was something. True, she had not seen much of America beyond the small private airport where the family jet had landed, or the dark night sky that had made it almost impossible to see this country where she suspected her brother had been his happiest. No, she'd mostly seen the Royal Hospital and then, the inside of Alejandro's house.

Thus far, she was underwhelmed by America.

She longed to do something besides tend to a frustratingly silent Alejandro or to defuse her father's angry outbursts. As much as she never thought she would say it, she missed Las Cruces. True, she had not been allowed to leave the estate's grounds, but within its securely patrolled borders, she'd had far more freedom than she'd had in Royal, Texas. She'd been able to chat with the maids and the cook. She'd been able to go to her workshop and work on her jewelry designs. She'd been able to saddle up Ixchel, her Azteca horse and, with Joaquin, ride wherever she pleased on Las Cruces' extensive grounds. It hadn't been true freedom. More like a reasonable facsimile of freedom.

But it was still more than what she had at the moment. Here, she was trapped with an invalid, an irate father and Joaquin, who, bless him, had never been much for conversation. The only break in the monotony had been the brief appearances of Maria, Alejandro's maid, as well as Nathan Battle, the local sheriff, and Bailey Collins, the state investigator who had been assigned to Alejandro's case.

Honestly, she wasn't sure how much longer she could stand it.

Gabriella wrapped the bandage around her finger, wishing she could wrap her head around the situation. For as long as she could remember, her world had been a safe, if constrained place. Now, with Alejandro's kidnapping, discovery and subsequent memory loss, everything was turned upside down.

In the midst of feeling sorry for herself, the doorbell chimed.

Perhaps Maria had returned. Gabriella liked talking to her. It was a relief to have a normal conversation with another woman, even if it was mere small talk about the weather and groceries. Anything to break up the monotony of the days in Alejandro's house.

She hurried out of the bathroom. Joaquin followed her to the door. They'd already reached an understanding that, in lieu of hiring more help—something her father was not interested in—Gabriella would answer the door and Joaquin would stand guard, ready to spring into action.

The bell chimed again, causing Gabriella to hurry. It couldn't be Maria—she wasn't that impatient. Which meant it was either the sheriff or the state investigator. Which meant her father would spend the better part of his afternoon raging at American injustices.

Resigned to her fate, Gabriella paused to catch her breath at the front door before opening it. She was, for the foreseeable future, the lady of the house. It was best to present the del Toro family in a positive light—all the more so because Maria had indicated that some members of the community were suspicious of the family of Alex Santiago. She checked her reflection in the hall mirror, thankful that the only thing out of place was the bandage on her finger, and affixed a warm smile to her face. She'd played the hostess for her father's business dinners before. She knew her role well.

Neither Sheriff Battle nor Agent Collins stood on the front stoop. Instead it was a cowboy—a tall, broad cowboy wearing a heathered sports jacket, a dark gray shirt and a dark pair of jeans over his gray ostrich cowboy boots. The moment he saw her, he whipped his brown felt hat off of his head and held it to his chest.

Oh. Green eyes. *¡Dios mío!* she had never seen eyes so green in her entire life. They were beautiful—the color of the spring grass at Las Cruces. For a moment looking into his eyes felt… It felt like coming home. His gaze affected her in a way she'd never before experienced.

"Howdy, ma'am." His voice was rough around the edges, as if he'd been outdoors in the February wind for some time. As he looked at her, one corner of his mouth crooked up, as if he were not surprised to see her, just pleased. "I'd like to talk to Alex, if he's up to it."

She was staring, she realized too late. Perhaps that was

because she hadn't seen too many outsiders recently. But the way this cowboy—for there could be no doubt that was what he was—was looking at her had rooted her to the spot.

His smile deepened as he held out one hand. "I'm Chance McDaniel. I don't believe I've had the pleasure, Miss…?"

Any homecoming died in the air between them. Chance McDaniel? What she knew of this man was limited, but it did nothing to endear him to her—or her father. According to Sheriff Battle and Agent Collins, Mr. McDaniel had been close friends with Alejandro—or rather, with Alex Santiago. However, he was also one of the leading suspects in Alejandro's disappearance—a crime of which he had not been cleared.

What was he doing here? More to the point, what was she going to do about it?

Behind her, Joaquin moved, his hand slipping up under his jacket. Gabriella quickly remembered herself. She could not imagine what would have led a leading suspect to ask to speak to the victim of a crime, but she also couldn't have Joaquin pulling a weapon on him. This wasn't Mexico, after all.

With a quick look that had Joaquin stopping in his tracks, Gabriella remembered her warm smile. "Hello, Mr. McDaniel. Won't you please enter?" Instead of shaking his outstretched hand, she stepped back, narrowly missing Joaquin, and motioned for Chance to enter.

He stood there for a beat too long before letting his hand fall to his side as he took long strides into the foyer. He moved with a confident ease, projecting strength with each step. Of course he was confident. Otherwise he wouldn't have dared ask to see Alejandro.

Upon seeing Joaquin glowering off to one side, Mr. McDaniel offered up a, "Howdy, *señor.*"

Behind his back, where he could not see it, a small smile danced across Gabriella's lips. She had not believed that real cowboys would actually speak in such colloquial language. It should have sounded ridiculous, but with Mr. McDaniel's rough-edged voice, it sent shivers down her spine.

Joaquin did not respond, of course. He stood like a statue at the edge of the room, his gaze trained on Mr. McDaniel.

Mr. McDaniel obviously knew his way around the house. He headed straight for the living room before seeming to remember himself. He paused and turned back to her. "I'm sorry, I didn't catch your name, Miss...?" As he said it, his gaze worked its way up and down Gabriella.

She could see him taking in her crisp white shirt—thankfully unstained with the failed efforts at lunch—and her slim black pants underneath the knee-length, coral-colored sweater-coat that contrasted perfectly with the heavy rope of turquoise and silver she wore around her neck, with earrings to match. He was trying to determine if she was the new housekeeper or not, Gabriella decided, as if every woman of Hispanic origins came to America to be a maid. However, she knew that very few maids dressed as she did. Which assumption would he go with?

If this man had been anyone other than the prime suspect in Alejandro's disappearance, she would have hurried to put him at ease. She decided to let him wait. After all, she'd had to wait to learn if her brother was even alive. Someone else should feel as anxious as she had, even for a solitary minute.

She said, "May I get you some tea?" in her nicest tone.

Instead of looking irritated or even uncomfortable, Mr. McDaniel gave her the kind of grin that he probably used to get the average woman to fall all over him. Well, he was about to learn that Gabriella was not the average woman, even if she did suddenly feel a bit unsettled at the warmth in his eyes. "Much obliged, ma'am."

Gabriella motioned him to the living room and then walked slowly and deliberately into the kitchen. Thankfully, making tea was her specialty and she already had a pitcher of iced tea steeping. It only took a minute to assemble a tray of two glasses and some biscuits. The whole time, she strained to hear any other noise coming from the house. If Alejandro had heard the door, he gave no indication of venturing downstairs to see who it was. But it also appeared that Papa had not heard the visitor arrive, which was probably for the best.

If Mr. McDaniel had had something to do with Alejandro's disappearance, there was a chance that Gabriella could "sweet talk" it out of him, as the Americans would say. If Papa stormed into the room and began making accusations, who knew what would happen?

She knew Papa would be furious that she had not let him handle the visitor personally. She was well-versed in the art of gentle conversation, after all, and had been told she was a beautiful woman on numerous occasions. She could handle a man like Chance McDaniel. Besides, it wasn't as if she was in actual danger. Joaquin was with her.

Mr. McDaniel had been sitting in the chair that faced Joaquin, apparently engaging in a staring match. But when Gabriella entered with the tray, he quickly stood. "Thank you for the tea."

Gabriella set the tray on the table, but neither of them made a move to pick up a glass. Instead she found herself staring at Chance McDaniel again, wondering what kind of man he was—the kind who would befriend a foreigner or the kind who would attack an unarmed man?

She sat in the leather armchair opposite the one he'd claimed. Joaquin moved forward to stand behind the back of her chair, an unmistakable warning in his presence. If this Mr. McDaniel tried anything, he wouldn't live to regret it.

A fact that he seemed to understand. Without another word, he sat, his gaze never leaving her face.

As she let the moment stretch, she again noted the way his presence left her feeling…unsettled. He'd dropped his hat on a side table. She could see his dark blond hair. He wore it quite short, but that apparently did nothing to stop the way it laid in waves on his head. He was freshly shaved but, aside from the boots and the hat, wore no other adornment.

He does not need any, she thought. The thought warmed her.

Finally he began to shift in his seat. She should not delay anymore, lest Papa burst into the room, ready to avenge his son.

"It is a pleasure to make your acquaintance, Mr. McDaniel. Alejandro had spoken of you to me." A touch of color deepened on Mr. McDaniel's cheeks. *¡Dios mío!* he was more than attractive. "I am Gabriella del Toro, Alejandro's sister."

This pronouncement hung in the air like a cloud ready to burst with rain. "I was not aware that Alex had a sister," he finally said. There was no mistaking the hurt undertone in his voice. "But then, I guess that there's plenty I didn't know about Alex. Like that his name is Alejandro." He looked to Joaquin over her shoulder. "Are you his brother, then?"

Gabriella laughed lightly. "Joaquin? No. He is my personal bodyguard. As I'm sure you can understand, Mr. McDaniel, the del Toro family must take every precaution."

Mr. McDaniel nodded. "How is he? Alex, I mean." He ran a hand over his hair. "I was hoping to talk to him, if he was feeling up to it."

Gabriella detected nothing deceptive in his voice or his

posture. "Alejandro is still recovering from his ordeal." Then, to Joaquin, she said, *"Devrions-nous dire à Papa première ou Alejandro qu'il est ici?"* in French. *Should we tell Papa first or Alejandro that he's here?*

She'd chosen French because she assumed that an American cowboy living in Texas probably spoke enough Spanish to catch what she said. Therefore, she was completely unprepared when Mr. McDaniel said, with great effort, *"Je peux dit moi"* in an accent that was so bad he was almost unintelligible. However, she was fairly certain he'd meant to say, *I can tell them myself.* What he'd actually said was, *I can tell me.*

Again, a smile crossed her lips. "You speak French."

More color came to his cheeks. She felt herself leaning forward to get a better look at him. "Not as beautifully as you do, but yeah, I took a couple of years in high school." His eyes twinkled. "My Spanish is better. I'm assuming that was the point?"

He had her. "Indeed," she admitted, impressed. A man who spoke in "howdys" and "ma'ams" who also conversed in Spanish and attempted French—with a sense of humor? With a compliment—she spoke French beautifully?

Gabriella could see how her brother would have befriended this man. Alejandro was drawn to people who had an easy way. She wasn't different, except that instead of making friends at work or on the social scene, that meant that she'd become fast friends with the hired help at Las Cruces.

What kind of cowboy was Chance McDaniel? Did he know how to ride? She glanced at his hands. They were clean, but rough with calluses. He was a man who was not afraid of hard work.

A shiver ran through her body. She thought she'd done a fine job of hiding it from Mr. McDaniel, but then his eyes widened and what had twinkled in them...changed. Deepened.

In that instant it became clear that Chance McDaniel was indeed a threat. To her, though—not necessarily her brother. Because the way that this man was looking at her—as though he was coming home, too—was something she had not expected.

Two

So Alex had a sister. Just another lie. Add it to the pile.

As mad as Chance wanted to be at the man he'd called friend, he couldn't quite get a grip on anger. Instead he was lost in the depths of chocolate-brown eyes.

Gabriella del Toro. He wanted to say her name out loud, to feel the way the syllables rolled over his tongue like single-malt whiskey. He didn't. Not now, anyway. The guy standing over her looked as though he might shoot Chance if he dared sully her name.

He needed to get back on track here. He knew the del Toro family had been in Alex's house for several weeks now—Nathan Battle had shared that over a drink at the Texas Cattleman's Club. But no other gossip had trickled down. Nathan was being tight-lipped about the whole damn thing, except to say that, as far as the local law was concerned, Chance was in the clear.

That meant the state investigator still considered him a suspect.

As did the del Toro family, apparently. Chance had to admit he was impressed. Gabriella del Toro may look like a polished socialite, but she'd made him sweat like a seasoned pro. He could only hope she hadn't realized how uncomfortable he'd been, what with that "personal body-guard" trying to kill him with looks alone.

This whole situation was still something he couldn't get his head around. Alex was back, safe and sound, but without much of an idea of who he was—hell, who anyone in Royal, Texas, was. The whole town was still on high alert, suspicious of anyone who might have ever had a bone to pick with Alex Santiago. This apparently included him.

"So, your bodyguard speaks French?" He honestly didn't know what else to say. He wanted to talk to Alex again; find out if he remembered anything else. As much as he hated to admit it, the odds were decent that someone in Royal had done this to his friend. The only other option was that Mexican drug violence was bleeding its way far north of the border.

"Of course," Gabriella said, as if every meathead in the world spoke several languages. "Since he joined me for my lessons, it was only natural that he learn with me and the other children at home."

"More brothers and sisters?" How could he have ever felt that he knew Alex? The man had done nothing but lie to him from the moment he'd arrived in Royal. Chance had thought he'd been friends with the man. Hell, he'd even done the honorable thing and stepped aside when Alex had showed an interest in Chance's lady friend, Cara Windsor. Or had that been part of the setup, too? Because if Alex had wanted to destroy Chance's life, he was doing a damn fine job of it.

"Oh, no, Mr. McDaniel." Gabriella had a soft laugh, delicate. Made him think of a butterfly landing quickly on a flower before moving on. "My tutors taught the children of our staff. We almost had enough students for a regular school." Her features softened. "My mother believed it was our duty to educate those who serve us."

Alex had never mentioned his mother. But then, he

hadn't mentioned a sister, either. "It must have been hard on your mother when Alex went missing."

A shadow crossed Gabriella's face, blocking out the light of her smile. "She has been dead for twenty-three years, Mr. McDaniel."

Okay, so maybe Alex had a good reason for not talking about his mother. "My apologies. I didn't know."

She tilted her head in appreciation, and then the shadow was gone. Her behavior was refined, her manners impeccable—even when she'd let him sweat, she'd been perfectly polite about it.

Chance was suddenly possessed—there wasn't another word for it—to ask if Gabriella rode horses. Alex had come out to McDaniel's Acres, Chance's homestead, to ride on numerous occasions. Alex had talked about his stables back home; how he'd always loved the freedom of riding.

Cara Windsor had never enjoyed riding with Chance. She didn't like the smell of the barn, had no particular talent for riding and was too terrified of being stepped on to consider brushing down a horse.

Chance had finished sowing his wild oats years ago. Since then, he'd worked on making McDaniel's Acres a profitable piece of land. He'd like to have someone to ride with him, someone to take his meals with—and share his bed with. But the land had taken all his time and there weren't too many women left in Royal who'd cotton to his way of life. Ranching the land—even if it was a dude ranch and the bunkhouse was now a five-star hotel where city folks paid a hefty price to be pretend cowboys for the week—was still a hard life, full of early summer mornings and cold winter nights.

"Do you ride horses?" Chance wouldn't have thought it possible, but the bodyguard's glare got meaner. "Alex would come out to the ranch and we'd ride."

He thought he saw a small smile ghost its way across Gabriella's very full lips. "I ride."

Two simple little words that had the immediate effect of cranking his temperature up a notch or two. "You should come out to the ranch sometime—McDaniel's Acres. This part of Texas is beautiful—the best way to see it is from horseback."

He wanted to think that he was asking only because he was concerned with clearing his name. If he couldn't talk with Alex and see what he remembered, the next best thing he could hope for was to talk with his beautiful sister. Maybe he could find out if anything about Alex had been on the level or if their entire friendship had been nothing but lies.

But he'd be lying if he didn't admit that spending some time out on the range with Gabriella had the potential to be fun.

"That would be out of the question, I'm afraid." She was back to blushing again, which made her look innocent. Which gave him some not-so-innocent thoughts. "I never go anywhere without Joaquin."

The big man grunted in agreement. Hey, what did Chance know—the bodyguard was capable of something besides glaring.

Chance made a snap decision. "He can come along. I've got a mule that can handle him. The more, the merrier." Which was a bold-faced lie, but he knew damn good and well that he wasn't going to find out anything today. "If you want," he added.

"How big is your ranch?" She leaned forward, causing the white shirt she was wearing to gape at the neck.

If Alex were here, he'd punch Chance in the arm for ogling his sister. As it was, Chance half expected to be shot. "About 400 acres. We've got cattle as well as some chickens, a few sheep and goats, and a few alpacas—the kids love them. And horses, of course. I run a dude ranch and hotel on the property," he added, hoping that made him sound more like a businessman making a pitch and less like a love-struck teenager angling for a date. "We give trail rides all the time. I'd be happy to show you around."

This was mostly true. He did lead trail rides—when it wasn't the middle of February. The winter hadn't held a great deal of snow to this point, but the wind could be vicious. He had no idea why he thought a ride with a re-fined woman such as Gabriella del Toro would be a good idea in this weather.

Oh, right—because he was hoping to find out some-thing more about Alex.

He hoped she'd say yes. He hoped she could handle her-self on a horse. Hell, he just hoped he wasn't about to be shot. Chance looked down at Gabriella's hands. Despite her polished appearance, he saw that her nails weren't long and manicured, but short and bare. Her hands were deli-cate, with long, thin fingers that showed signs of heavy use—and a bandage on her index finger. "Did you hurt yourself?"

That pink blush graced her cheeks. She dropped her gaze, but then looked up at him through thick lashes. "Just a cut. I was attempting to prepare some soup for Alejan-dro."

Attempting? He grinned at her. "When you come out for a ride, we'll have dinner. Franny Peterson is the best cook in Royal—she makes dinner for my guests. She'd be delighted to meet Alex's family. They always got along famously."

Her smile tightened. "Alejandro often visited your home?"

"Yup."

"Was he…?" She looked down at her bandaged hand, unable to finish the sentence.

This must be so hard on her, he realized. Then he remembered—he hadn't come here to flirt with Alex's sister, no matter how fun it might become. He had a purpose here. "How is he? Any better?"

Everything that had been warm and light about Gabriella shut down on him. She didn't so much as move, but he felt the walls that went up between them.

Gabriella said, "He is much the same," in a voice that was probably supposed to sound as though she wasn't giving anything away. But he heard the sadness in her tone.

Gabriella appeared to care for her brother. For some reason, that made Chance happy. He didn't know why.

"Can I see him?"

Joaquin stiffened behind her as Gabriella said, "I do not think that would be wise, Mr. McDaniel. He is still healing. The doctors have said he needs quiet and darkness for his brain to recover from the trauma he's suffered."

"Mr. McDaniel is my father. Call me Chance. Everyone does. Even Alex."

Then she looked up at him, the full force of her brown eyes boring into him. "I do not think that would be wise, Mr. McDaniel."

Hell, he'd overstepped, but he couldn't figure out which thing had been too far. He couldn't tell which part had pushed her over the edge. Was it the familiarity of using his given name—or of calling Alex by his American name? Whatever it had been, he was losing her. "I just thought that if he, you know, saw me, it might jog his memory. He might remember who I was."

Lots of women had cried on Chance's shoulder in his time—he was the kind of guy that women felt comfortable enough with that they could occasionally pour their hearts out to him. But when Gabriella del Toro lifted her gaze to his face, he was sure he'd never seen a sadder woman in his life.

"I had hoped that, as well."

It shouldn't have bothered him this much—he had known Gabriella for all of twenty minutes. But the pain in her voice cut right through him and, just like that, he felt the same way he'd felt when he'd first heard that Alex had gone missing—as though a part of him had been hacked off with a rusty saw.

He wanted to go to her, offer her a sympathetic shoulder to lean on. He wanted her to know that, despite what she might have heard, he'd had nothing to do with Alex's disappearance—that he only wanted what was best for his friend. And his friend's family.

But he also didn't want to bleed today. So instead of risking the wrath of Joaquin the bodyguard, he pulled his wallet out of his back pocket and fished out one of his seldom-used business cards. It was a little worn around the edges because he needed them so rarely. Everyone in Royal knew him and how to get ahold of him.

But if Alex couldn't remember Chance—couldn't remember his own sister—then there was zero point in expecting him to tell Gabriella what Chance's phone number was. He held the card out to her. "If anything changes—if you need my help in any way, here's my number. I can be here in twenty minutes if Alex needs me." He swallowed, hoping he wasn't about to find himself thrown out of the house. "If you need me."

She stood. For a moment he thought she would once again tell him that she didn't think that a wise idea, but then she took the offered card. Her fingertips grazed the edge of his—a small touch, but one that made him want to smile again. "Thank you."

"Who are you?" a voice thundered from behind him. Then he asked the same thing in Spanish. *"¿Quién es?"*

Chance barely caught the look of alarm on Gabriella's face before he spun around to see the man who could only be Alex's father filling the kitchen doorway. The older man stood with his feet spread, his hands on his hips and his chest puffed up. He was nearly as tall as Chance was—maybe a few inches shorter than Alex. He could have been Alex's twin, if it weren't for the lines etched into his forehead. Same black hair, same build—but the face was all different. Alex had an easy smile and warm eyes—the kind of guy a man could knock back a beer or two with on a Friday night.

This was not a man who probably ever knocked back a couple of beers. No doubt about it, this was the senior del Toro. Rodrigo. Nathan had said the old man was a force to be reckoned with. He hadn't been lying.

"Papa," Gabriella said in a soft—but not weak—voice. "This is Chance McDaniel, Alejandro's friend."

He sure did appreciate her putting it in those terms, as opposed to mentioning that he was also the lead suspect in Alex's disappearance.

Not that she needed to. Rodrigo's eyes blazed with an undisguised hatred at Chance's name. *"¿Qué está haciendo aquí?"* he snarled as Gabriella went to stand next to her father. Chance felt Joaquin come up behind him; probably just close enough to grab Chance if he made a funny move.

What was Chance doing here? Rodrigo must not be as perceptive as his daughter. Gabriella had assumed that Chance spoke Spanish, but Rodrigo had incorrectly assumed Chance did not. So he said, *"Hola, Señor del Toro. Alex hablaba bien de usted." Alex spoke well of you.*

Or at least, that's what he hoped he'd said. Alex had always spoken in crisp English, much the way Gabriella did. Chance had never had private tutors, unless one counted the hired hands on the ranch—and they'd spent more time teaching him to cuss in Spanish than to make polite greetings.

When this didn't get him shot, he added in his most polite business voice that he had come to see Alex. And he made damn sure not to flinch in Joaquin's direction when the big man huffed. This would be a bad time to show any sign of nerves or fear. So Chance kept his face calm and his gaze steady. He may be a cowboy, by God, but he was a McDaniel and no one—not even Rodrigo del Toro—was going to stare him down.

Then he saw the corners of Gabriella's mouth curve into a small smile. Even if Rodrigo hated his guts, at the very least, Chance had said what she'd wanted to hear.

"You are not welcome in this house," Rodrigo said, switching back to English. His accent was thicker, less crisp—but his words flowed easily.

"Papa," Gabriella said as she put a hand on his arm.

"Gabriella," he shot back. She pulled her hand away and cast her gaze to the ground. "You are not welcome in this house," he repeated, his voice a notch louder.

That did it. Chance could handle a man trying to bullshit him, but to speak to his daughter in such a callous manner? Nope. Not happening. "Last I heard, this was still Alex's house and I'd bet dollars to doughnuts that I've spent more time here than you have. I'm welcome here until Alex says otherwise." He saw the look of alarm on Gabriella's face. *"Señor,"* he said in his most dismissive voice.

Still, he wasn't stupid. He'd worn out his welcome in a big way. Before Joaquin could grab him by the scruff of his neck, he snatched his hat off the side table. "Ms. del Toro, it was a pleasure to meet you." He then turned to Joaquin and was unsurprised to see the man's fists swinging by his sides. "Keep up the good work, Joaquin."

He heard footsteps behind him and tensed, expecting a blow of some kind. He was surprised, however, when Gabriella slipped past him to reach the door before him. She opened it and stood to the side with a confused look on her face. "I will tell Alejandro you stopped by," she said.

Chance glanced back over his shoulder. Joaquin was fewer than five feet away—for a big man, he could move like a cat when he wanted to, apparently. Rodrigo del Toro had not moved from the doorway, though. He stood there with his arms crossed, glaring as if he possessed laser vision or something. Chance couldn't help himself. He tipped his hat to the older man, knowing it'd piss him off.

Then he turned back to Gabriella. "I hope he won't be too mad." That got him a worried smile telling him exactly how bad Rodrigo would be after he left. "Call me for anything. The offer to ride stands."

She did not meet his gaze, but he saw the delicate pink that rushed to her cheeks.

"Gabriella," Rodrigo roared.

"Goodbye, Mr. McDaniel." She shut the door behind him.

Chance walked out to his truck and then turned to look at Alex's house. He didn't see Alex's face in any of the upper windows.

He had a feeling he'd be hearing from Gabriella. Maybe not today, maybe not tomorrow—but soon. The way her eyes had lit up when he'd talked about riding the range? Yeah, she was going to call—especially if she was stuck in that house with a silent shadow of a bodyguard and a raging father. Not to mention a brother who didn't remember her.

He hoped Gabriella was as good as her word and told Alex that Chance had come by.

That would make her better than her brother.

Because as of now, his word meant nothing to Chance.

Three

It took four days before Chance's cell phone rang. He'd just gotten back to the barn from checking on the ponds for the cattle. When his phone rang, it played Alex's ringtone. For a moment Chance thought it was Alex; that he had his memory back, that he wanted to tell Chance about everything—which may or may not include his sister.

He handed Ranger, his horse, to Marty and grabbed his phone out of its holster. "Hello?"

"Ah, yes—Mr. McDaniel?"

Gabriella's soft voice flowed around him. Chance was simultaneously disappointed that it wasn't Alex and thrilled that she'd called. "I told you to call me Chance, Gabriella."

There was something of an awkward pause. He could almost see her trying to decide if she was going to call him what he wanted her to. Because he sure as hell wanted to hear what her accent would do with his name.

But it didn't look as if it was going to happen right now, so he redirected the conversation. "Any change in Alex?"

"No. He is still…resting." She sounded not awesome, frankly. Tired and worried, but underneath that, he could hear frustration. She was doing a damn fine job hiding it, but he could still tell.

"Is your father still mad at me?"

"Papa is only concerned with Alejandro's well-being." Her answer came without hesitation. In fact, it almost sounded as though she'd rehearsed it.

He grinned. That was a *yes,* loud and clear. "So, you need to get out of the house for a while? I've got a beauty of a quarter horse named Nightingale that'd love to ride you around."

She didn't say anything at first, but he heard her sigh— a sound of relief. Oh, yeah—he had her.

His mind hurried to put images with the sounds coming across his phone. He could see her full, red lips slightly parted as she exhaled, see her thick lashes fluttering at the thought of going for a ride with him.

Then, because apparently he enjoyed torturing himself, his mind turned those images in a different direction—her smooth hair all mussed up against a pillow as he coaxed little noises out of her. As she rode *him.*

He went hard in his jeans at the thought.

"You said you had a mule for Joaquin?"

"Yup." Chance walked down the aisle of his barn and stopped in front of Beast's stall. The animal was a giant mule that came from a donkey crossed with a draft horse. Beast's mother had been a Belgian, which meant he was a solid seventeen hands high and built like a tank.

Chance had found that having a larger animal around meant more guests could take a trail ride—something that they'd appreciated. Most trail rides capped rider weight around two hundred fifty pounds, maybe a bit more. Beast let some folks who'd never been allowed on a horse to take their first ride—which was good for business. "This fellow can handle up to three fifty. Shouldn't be a problem—if Joaquin eats a small breakfast, that is."

She laughed at this and again Chance was reminded of

butterflies fluttering among the spring flowers. "I'll be sure to tell him that."

"When do you want to come out?" It was Thursday. The weekend was suddenly looking up. By a lot. "The forecast is calling for clear skies for the next few days."

"When are you available?"

Hell, he was available anytime she wanted him to be. But then Marty walked over and said, in a quiet voice, "Don't forget the wedding Saturday."

Damn. It was February, after all. The dude ranch business may have slowed down, but the destination wedding business was still moving along at a decent clip. "We're hosting a wedding on Saturday night for a party from Houston." Double damn it. Saturday would have been a great time to get to know Gabriella a little better—or at least to figure out if all the del Toros lied as much as Alex did. "How about…?" His mind spun. Saturday was out. "Sunday afternoon?"

"That would not be possible." He couldn't help but notice that she hadn't said, "Mr. McDaniel." Of course, she also hadn't said, "Chance." Still, it was progress. "It is Sunday, after all."

Ah. He hadn't considered that. Alex had gone to the local Catholic church on occasion, but the way Gabriella said it made it clear that she was more than just an occasional churchgoer. Did that make her more honest than her brother? Or just more guilty when she lied?

He could feel this opportunity slipping through his fingers. There was no way in hell Rodrigo del Toro would let him back in the house, which meant this was the only way possible to find out what the hell was going on.

That only left him with one choice. "How about tomorrow morning? We'll be setting up for a wedding, but I've got a good crew. We can head out around…say, ten, then have lunch?"

Say yes, he thought. *Please say yes.* God, how he wanted to know if she rode or if she was the kind of "rider" who just thought horses were pretty.

She was silent, but that didn't mean everything was quiet on her end. Although it was faint, he was pretty sure he heard Rodrigo shout, "Gabriella!" followed by a string of Spanish that Chance couldn't make out.

"Ten tomorrow," she said simply before the call ended.

Chance grinned down at his phone. He knew he needed to keep his eyes peeled and his defenses up. Alex had screwed him over pretty damn badly and while McDaniel's Acres was still operating in the black, he hadn't had as much local business because of all the rumors.

He needed to find out what Alex remembered. That had to be his first goal tomorrow. It should be his only goal, too. Tomorrow should have nothing to do with wanting to hear Gabriella's tongue roll over his name, *nothing* to do with wanting to roll his own tongue over a few other things. This was about clearing his name, damn it.

Still. She'd called. They were going to ride.

Yup. The weekend was looking much better.

Gabriella was up early the next morning. She was usually up by six-thirty, but today she was out of bed at a quarter to six.

She would have liked to have had a cup of coffee without waking Joaquin, but as he slept in the living room—the better to hear anyone breaking in—she had no choice but to get him up early.

"*Buenos días,* Joaquin," she said the moment she entered the living room. Joaquin did not appreciate people trying to sneak past him. The first time she'd tried that—she'd been fifteen and dying to get out of the house—he'd grabbed her by the calf so hard that she'd had bruises for weeks. He'd apologized profusely, of course—he had been dead asleep and had not realized it was his charge sneaking around instead of a villain.

Without hesitation, Joaquin sat up from the couch, his eyes already alert as he scanned the room.

"I awoke early," she explained as he removed his gun from underneath the pillow he'd been sleeping on and slid it back into its holster. "Nothing is wrong. Coffee?"

Joaquin nodded and scrubbed a hand over his face. Then he stood and began his morning perimeter check, prowling around the house as silent as a breeze, checking the locks and windows. Of course Alejandro had had a security system installed, but security systems could always be bypassed. Gabriella knew he wouldn't attend to any of his needs until he was confident the del Toro family was safe.

Gabriella made the coffee extra strong. She was excited about the day in a way that she had not felt since she'd convinced Papa to allow her to accompany him north to America.

Finally she was going to see something of Texas—something more than the lovely vista visible through Alejandro's windows. From horseback, no less! Back home at Las Cruces, she'd ridden every day. In the few weeks she'd been here, she hadn't seen a horse. Stir-crazy, she thought was the American phrase for it. Because that's what she was. And that's why she was up before the sun.

Joaquin appeared in the kitchen. He accepted his mug of coffee and sat at the table, his tablet in front of him. Joaquin was forever scanning news sites, looking for any information that might pose a threat to the del Toro family.

But he didn't power the device up. Instead, as he sipped his coffee, he looked at Gabriella.

She knew that look. True, Joaquin was not much of a talker, but he'd been with her long enough that he rarely had to say anything to communicate with her. Right now, he was wondering if he should let her go for a ride with Chance McDaniel.

"Maria will be by today to straighten up," Gabriella said defensively. "She'll be preparing a week's worth of dinners. If Alejandro needs me, she knows how to get ahold of me. And Papa will be here. Alejandro will not be alone."

Joaquin raised an eyebrow. It wasn't enough to convince him, so she went on. "You heard what Mr. McDaniel said—he has over 400 acres of land. We're merely seeing if there's anywhere he could have hidden Alejandro away for a few weeks. An outbuilding or an abandoned cabin, perhaps."

That got her an even more skeptical look. Joaquin was clearly thinking that the local law enforcement had probably already scoured the land and had turned up nothing.

Gabriella sighed in frustration. If she couldn't convince Joaquin, there was no hope in convincing her father. "We'll be having lunch," she went on, hoping to sound like a dispassionate investigator instead of a younger version of herself, chafing at the restrictions that kept her safe. "I'll have the chance to talk with his staff, see if they have anything to say about him or Alejandro."

Joaquin shook his head, a motion of pity.

Fine. Have it your way, she thought. "If I don't get out of this house—even for a morning—I will make your day a living hell, Joaquin. I will make you help organize my closet and debate a new hairstyle and do some online shopping and I will ask you if you think those pants make my bottom look large. And then I will experiment with new ingredients in the kitchen and ask you to try the new soup or the new dessert. Is that what you want?"

She did not often throw a fit. She was no longer the headstrong thirteen-year-old who had rebelled whenever she could. She had accepted her lot, wrapped in a cocoon of safety, at her father's command. His only concern was her well-being, after all.

Her well-being depended on a few hours away from her family. That was that.

She leaned back on the counter and waited. She knew that her attempts at cooking usually resulted in a smoke alarm going off. Plus, like any self-respecting male, forcing Joaquin to give his opinion on clothing and hairstyles ranked just below being shot. If she tried hard—and started trying on shoes—she could make him wish someone would kill him just to put him out of his misery.

She got out the bowls and the cereal before she set the milk on the table. "Perhaps I shall try pancakes again," she mused. "They weren't *that* bad last time, were they?"

They had, of course, been horrid—not even the dogs would eat them. They'd been less "cake" and more "biscuit" in texture—and of course she'd burned them. Papa and Alejandro had gamely tried them, as had Joaquin, who had suffered from indigestion for the next two days.

Joaquin shot her a surprisingly dirty look as he rubbed his chest. Clearly he was remembering the indigestion, as well. "I will kill him if he touches you," he said, his voice creaky from lack of use.

Gabriella smiled. She'd broken him, which was no mean feat in and of itself. Joaquin was trained to resist torture, but no technique could defend against her attempts at cooking. "Of course," she agreed, trying to contain her excitement. "Papa would expect nothing less."

She finished her cold breakfast and went up to shower. Her heart was racing as she dressed and braided her hair back into a long, secure rope.

She wanted to get to McDaniel's Acres as soon as possible, but she had one thing to do first.

Gabriella assembled a tray with not-too-burned toast, cold cereal, orange juice and a thermos of coffee and headed upstairs. She juggled the tray and knocked on the door. "Alejandro? It's me. Gabriella."

The door cracked open and Alejandro stood in front of her. He gave her a look that made her wonder if her knew who she was. He wore a rumpled white tee and plaid pajama bottoms.

Nothing had changed. Oh, how she wished that one day he'd wake up and be her brother again. She lifted his breakfast. "I brought you food. Are you hungry?"

Alejandro stared at her a moment longer, as if he wasn't seeing her but through her. "Thank you," he mumbled, stepping to the side so she could enter.

The room was a disaster. The sheets were in a heap on the floor, socks were everywhere and the television was on the blue screen. It looked as though Alejandro hadn't left this room in weeks—because he hadn't. "Your housekeeper, Maria, will be here today. She'll prepare you lunch and tidy up this room. She will also do any laundry you require."

This announcement was met with Alejandro slumping back onto his bed, staring at the blue screen.

Gabriella set his tray down and gathered up the remains of last night's dinner. It hurt her to see her brother like this. At first, she'd been so relieved that he'd been found, but without his memory, it was almost as if he were still lost. Right in front of her, but still lost.

"I'm going to be visiting your old friend, Chance McDaniel, today," she said, more to keep the tears at bay than anything else.

Then something unusual happened. Alejandro's head snapped up and his eyes focused on her. For the first time in weeks, she felt as if he knew who she was. Or, at the very least, who Mr. McDaniel was.

Was that it? Did he remember something about Chance McDaniel—something connected with his abduction?

Just as her hopes began to rise, he said, "Everyone keeps talking about him, but…" He shrugged his shoulders and looked away.

This time, however, she wasn't so sure that he didn't know. His gaze had been too direct, too knowing. "He invited me out to ride at his ranch," she continued, busying herself with gathering up his dirty clothes—and keeping a close eye on him. "Joaquin will be joining me, of course."

Her brother was stroking his chin now, looking thoughtful—and very aware.

"Papa agreed," Gabriella went on, fluffing his pillows. "He thought it would give me the chance to see if Mr. McDaniel has any place where he could hide a person."

Out of the corner of her eye, she saw him shake his head. It was a small gesture, but it seemed as if Alejandro thought this little mission was foolish.

Gabriella couldn't contain herself any longer. She fell on her knees in front of Alejandro, taking his hands in hers. "If you could tell me anything—something you remember, some sound, *something*—I will help you." That unfocused blankness stole back over his face. "Don't you trust me, *hermano*?"

At first she did not think he was going to respond. But then he disentangled his hands from hers and patted her on the cheek. "You are…"

Gabriella's throat closed up. Did he remember her?

"You are a nice lady," he finished. "Have fun riding."

Then he was gone, flopping back onto his bed and grabbing the remote. Within seconds, the sounds of football filled the room.

Gabriella stood, blinking hard against the tears in her eyes. If he was in there—and, for the first time in days, she had hope that he was—then one thing was painfully clear.

He didn't trust her.

Gabriella pulled the door shut behind her and paused to

collect herself. Alejandro had managed to say something to her, after all. If he suspected Mr. McDaniel had had a part in his kidnapping, surely he would not have told her to have fun riding with the man.

But he had. She was a nice lady, whatever that meant, and she should have fun.

So that was exactly what she was going to do.

Four

With Joaquin in the driver's seat, Gabriella arrived at McDaniel's Acres at 9:55 a.m. They drove under the rustic gate that welcomed visitors before they continued up a long, winding drive of blacktop.

Gabriella leaned close to the tinted windows in the backseat, trying to take in the magnitude of the land they were crossing.

Hills rolled in all directions. Clusters of trees followed what was probably an arroyo or creek, but there weren't the old-growth forests that ringed Las Cruces. Instead low shrubs and those famous tumbleweeds dotted the landscape.

What would the hills look like in a few months? Would Texas bluebells cover the ground, color exploding everywhere? Or would grass grow in, deep and green—like Chance McDaniel's eyes?

She straightened in her seat and glanced at Joaquin's silent form in the front seat. She was not here to think about Mr. McDaniel's eyes and she would not be here in a few months to see the spring bloom. She would be back at Las Cruces, riding her own horses and making jewelry and not attempting more pancakes under any circumstances. Alejandro would be safe and things could go back to normal. That was what she wanted, wasn't it? Everything to return to normal?

She thought back to her conversation with Alejandro. This was the most animated she'd seen him since...since Papa had told him they would all be returning to Las Cruces as soon as the hospital had released Alejandro. Alejandro had snapped to life for a brief moment to say that under no circumstances was he leaving his home or Royal, Texas. Then he had lapsed back into his blank silence.

What if Alejandro did not want things to return to normal? What if, despite his abduction, he wished to stay in America?

That may very well be the case. But why? That was the question that Gabriella had little hope of answering on her own.

She smiled. Today, she was not on her own. She was going riding—with her brother's stilted blessing—with Chance McDaniel. She would find out as much as she could about her brother's life in Texas—and about Mr. McDaniel himself.

Joaquin slowed as they approached a sign. Its four arms pointed in two directions. The Bunk House, Swimming Pool and Deliveries pointed west; Trail Rides pointed north. Joaquin kept heading straight north.

Off to the west, she could see a large building that appeared to be made out of rough-hewed logs. It stood three stories tall, with a wide porch that looked as though it probably saw a great deal of activity during the summer. Even from this distance, she could see workers hanging garlands from the beams. *Those must be for the wedding,* she thought. It looked lovely, but if she were to get married here, she'd make sure to wait for the spring bloom.

Then the road took them farther away from the house and deeper into the ranch. A series of buildings appeared. Within moments, they were parked in front of a massive barn, its bright red color a beacon in the otherwise gray surroundings. Several smaller buildings were arranged behind the red barn. Some horses were loose in paddocks around the barns, some were scratching against posts. They all had that fuzzy look of animals in late winter.

Joaquin pulled up next to a deep blue pickup, got out and came around to open Gabriella's door for her. Upon exiting the vehicle, she walked over to where one horse was rubbing its head on a post. "Itchy?" she asked, and was rewarded by the horse—a palomino—leaning his head into her hands.

Gabriella smiled as some of the weight seemed to lift itself off of her shoulders. The breeze, while cool, felt fresh on her face—hinting at the spring that was coming. The horse groaned in appreciation as she rubbed his ears. A great deal of fur was coming off in her hands, but she didn't mind. Oh, how she had missed her horses—the smell was enough to lift her spirits.

"Lucky horse," a deep, slightly raspy voice said from behind her.

Gabriella spun to see Chance McDaniel tying a horse to a hitching post. His fingers moved smoothly, but his eyes were trained on her.

Oh, she thought with a small gasp. The man who had come to the door a few days ago had looked like a cowboy, yes—but almost a formal one. But the man who stood in front of her today? Pure cowboy. He wore a denim shirt under a light brown barn jacket. She was sure he was wearing jeans, but they were obscured by the worn black leather chaps that hugged his legs. Those weren't show chaps—no, the leather had that broken-in look that said he'd worn them often. Daily. The hat was the only thing that was the same—brown felt.

That and his eyes. The green was more vivid than she remembered. And the way he looked at her? Not as if he was a wolf and she the lamb. Too many men had looked at her that way—as though she was to be sacrificed on the altar of her father's business, a merger to be made between bottom lines and not between hearts.

No, Chance McDaniel looked at her without a single dollar sign in his eyes. Instead there was something else. Something that was almost… Well, certainly *not* joy at seeing her. That would not be possible. Nonetheless, it was something that made her body warm, despite the breeze.

Gabriella could not help the wide smile that broke over her face. "Mr. McDaniel."

He notched an eyebrow in clear challenge. "What's it going to take to get you to call me Chance, Gabriella?"

Her name sounded differently when he said it—gone were the smoothly flowing vowel sounds. Instead he stretched the *ah* into a harder *a*. It should have sounded grating, but she liked the rougher sound. No one else spoke her name like that. Just him.

Joaquin stepped in front of Gabriella before she could formulate a proper response to Chance McDaniel's familiarities.

"Howdy, Joaquin." Again, Chance was not seemingly put out by the bodyguard's presence. "Let me go get Beast." Then he patted the beautiful roan quarter horse he'd hitched to the post. "This here is Nightingale— although we call her Gale for short. I hope you like her."

Then, with a little nod of his head, he turned and headed back to the barn.

Joaquin gave her a look that said, *Is he for real?*

Gabriella responded by shrugging. It would be lovely if Chance McDaniel was "real." She reached into her pocket and pulled out the bag of carrot bits she'd mutilated in the kitchen last night. She walked up to Gale and held out a carrot. Gale sniffed, then snatched the treat.

"Ah, hello," she said as Gale sniffed her hair. "Would

you like another?" She palmed another carrot, which Gale all but inhaled. "That's a good girl."

She heard the sound of hooves—large hooves—clomping on the ground. Gabriella looked up to find Chance staring at her. That warmth coursed through her body again, but she wasn't about to let anyone know that. Not even the horse. "Yes?"

"Making friends?"

"But of course." Gabriella's cheeks flushed hot as he continued to stare at her. "It worked," she added as Gale nudged her with her nose.

Then she noticed the animal he was leading. Gale was perhaps sixteen hands high, but the mule—Beast, Chance had said—made the quarter horse look like a child's pony. It wasn't that the animal was that much taller than Gale, for he wasn't, perhaps another hand—no more than four more inches. But Beast clearly outweighed the quarter horse—perhaps by as much as half a ton.

She gasped, more than a little afraid of an animal that large.

Chance grinned at her. "Nothing to be scared of. Beast is as gentle as a kitten." He patted the big animal's neck before giving Gabriella a look that had nothing to do with horses. "You should make friends with him, too."

Far more than her cheeks flushed as Gabriella took a few hesitant steps toward Beast. His long ears—almost twice as long as Gale's—swiveled toward her. "*Hola,* Beast," she said, holding out a carrot on the flat of her palm. She'd long ago learned it was best to keep her hand as flat as possible. Holding a carrot or a sugar cube by her fingertips had gotten her nipped quite badly on the finger when she'd been six.

Beast's enormous lips scraped the carrot off of her hand, causing her to giggle. "You're a good boy, aren't you?"

"One of the best," Chance agreed. He was almost shoulder to shoulder with her, his voice far smoother than she'd heard it yet.

One of Beast's plate-size feet stamped at the earth, which caused Gabriella to jump. If she hadn't known any better, she would have thought she'd felt the shock waves from the impact. Chance laughed. "He likes you," he said, that twinkle in his eye.

"How can you tell?" She'd been stepped on by horses before, but Beast looked as if he would break every bone in her foot. She was in no mood to find out.

"If he didn't, he'd back up. He's predictable like that." Chance handed the reins to Joaquin. "There's a mounting block over there." Then he turned to Gabriella, that same twinkle shining brightly. "Let me help you up."

He crouched next to Gale's side and laced his fingers together. Gabriella hesitated—she could swing into the saddle by herself—but if she wanted to make friends with Chance, she needed to be friendly. So she placed her foot in his hand and let him boost her up onto the horse's back. Once she was in the saddle, he put his hand on her calf, right above her riding boot, and guided her foot into the stirrup.

Her breath caught at the too-familiar touch. She hardly knew this man and still had not ascertained if he was a danger to Alejandro or to her—but the way his hand had felt strong and sure against her leg had not felt like a risk. Instead it had felt…safe. Which was ridiculous. She did not need his help getting settled into the saddle. He started around to the other side of the horse, but Gabriella quickly put her foot in the stirrup.

Then he untied the reins and handed them to her. "Be right back," he said, leaving her in a state of unfamiliar confusion.

People, as a rule, did not touch her. To do so was to invite Joaquin to beat them senseless. And yet, Chance

SARAH M. ANDERSON   45

McDaniel had put his hands on her as if it were the most natural thing in the world.

She turned the horse until she could see Joaquin, who had indeed used the mounting block and was now sitting astride Beast. He gave her a look that said, "Are you okay?"

"I am fine," she replied, although she wasn't sure how true that was. "You?"

Joaquin looked down at the ground and managed to nod his head.

"You okay up there, big guy?" Chance came trotting out of the barn on a dappled gelding. When Joaquin nodded again, Chance asked, "What do you ride at home?"

"Joaquin rides an Andalusian and I prefer my Azteca, Ixchel."

"I know what an Andalusian is, but what's an Azteca?" As he asked, he pointed his horse away from the barn. Gabriella fell in stride next to him, with Joaquin bringing up the rear.

"A mix of Andalusian, quarter horse and Mexican crillo," she explained. "Ixchel is a paint. She is a well-trained animal. I always wanted to show her, but…" That had been another source of rebellion when she'd been fourteen and fifteen. Other girls in her social circle were making weekend trips to competitions and talking of Olympic dreams—all activities that were forbidden to Gabriella.

"Why didn't you?" Chance kept his gaze forward. His posture was relaxed, but she could hear something in his voice that was far more than casual curiosity.

"Papa said that the competitions were not secure enough and he could not guarantee my safety if I went."

That got a reaction out of him. "Beg pardon?"

"Joaquin is an excellent bodyguard, but in a crowded space filled with horses and people, he cannot control the situation the way he can at Las Cruces. That's our family estate," she hurried to add.

"Wait, so—are you telling me that you don't have a bodyguard because of what happened to Alex?"

She could not decide if she liked the confusion in his voice. On the one hand, it was quite clear that Chance McDaniel had not known that—which was good because it meant that he had not done any surveillance or research into the del Toro family's comings and goings.

However, on the other hand, the way Chance said it made it clear that the idea of constant security sounded like more than a little overkill.

"Joaquin has been with me for fourteen years," she said, knowing that would only add fuel to Chance's curiosity.

"Are you serious?"

"Of course. Mexico is not a safe place for the wealthy. People are kidnapped for exorbitant ransoms. It's a business."

He appeared to mull over this information as the trail lead them farther and farther away from the buildings. "Is that normal, then? To have a bodyguard for a decade and a half?"

"Oh, I have had a guard my entire life. Papa hired Joaquin after he bested my former guard, Raul."

She felt as if she might be giving too much away— this was the sort of information that could be used to help formulate an abduction—but it didn't feel as though she was feeding him the things he wanted to know. Instead he seemed genuinely shocked.

"What do you mean, 'bested'?" His voice was level, but there was no mistaking the concern.

She warmed at his tone. Perhaps she shouldn't find it comforting that he was worried about her. Perhaps this was him on a fact-finding mission about how the del Toro family operated.

But she didn't think so. "All of the guards in our family

have to withstand tests, if you will, of their ability to keep us safe. If they fail in their mission, they are replaced."

Chance pulled his horse to an abrupt stop, which caused her horse to stop, as well. "What?" His tone was not pleased.

"It is not as bad as it sounds." But this defense didn't strike her as being particularly truthful.

"Doesn't that scare the hell out of you?"

She couldn't meet his gaze. "Usually the attempts are not very serious."

"But not always."

"No," she replied softly. "Not always."

The last time, the "pretend" kidnappers had taken their assignment a bit too seriously. Gabriella had been driving into Mexico City to meet with a gallery owner about showing her latest collection of jewelry when… Of course, their car was completely bulletproof, so Gabriella had not been in real danger. Or so she told herself time and time again.

"How bad was it?"

The sound of Chance's voice—low and with a slight rasp to it—called her back from her fear. She looked into his eyes and again was struck with that odd sense of coming home. "Joaquin defended me with honor—as he always does."

"How many times has this happened?"

The look on Chance's face wouldn't let her go. He was serious but underneath that was a different emotion—fury. "Usually once a year."

Chance let loose with a string of curse words quite unlike anything Gabriella had ever heard—at least, not all at once. The sudden explosion of sound should have been alarming but instead Gabriella found herself grinning and then giggling. She cast a glance back at Joaquin, who was as impassive as ever.

"—lower than a rattler's belly in a wagon rut!" Chance

finished with a flourish. "Can you tell me why, on God's green earth, a man would do that to his own daughter?"

"He had Alejandro's guards tested, as well," she told him, wondering when she had become the focus of his attention—and wondering if that was necessarily a warning sign. If it was, surely Joaquin would have rounded on Chance by now.

That statement did not seem to appease Chance's temper. "You've got to be pulling my chain. *Why?*"

He didn't know. She found a measure of relief in that— the more time she spent with Chance, the less she suspected him in Alejandro's disappearance. Or, at the very least, the less she suspected him of targeting the del Toro family for its fortune. He may have still had a hand in Alejandro's disappearance, but she could not believe that he had known that Alex Santiago was Alejandro del Toro.

Gabriella opened her mouth to tell him, but the words wouldn't come. The memories were too hard to deal with, even after twenty-three years. But he sat there, still, those beautiful eyes of his staring at her, expecting an answer.

When she could not give him one, she turned her horse back up the trail and urged her to a fast walk.

Apparently, Chance was in no mood to let her walk away from him—even if it was on horseback. He came level with her in moments, his mount easily keeping pace with Gale. "Who?" he asked, his tone more gentle than before.

"Our mother," she replied, trying to keep her own voice level. She couldn't risk a glance at him, though, so she kept her eyes focused on the land around them. "According to the police, she was killed when she tried to escape." Very few kidnappings ended that way—dead people were worth nothing, while living people were worth money. And wasn't money the whole point?

But Elena del Toro had not been a docile victim. "She

had fought them." That point made Gabriella proud of her mother but, at the same time, it infuriated her. Elena had not gone as meek as a church mouse—but if she had, would she still be here? Would everything have been different?

Would Gabriella have more than a few hazy memories of her own mother?

"When?"

"I was four. Alejandro was eight." She'd always been jealous of Alejandro. He had memories that Gabriella never would, after all. He remembered birthdays and Christmases, trips to visit Tía Manuela and church. All Gabriella had was a random collection of images, the strongest of which had always been of helping her mother choose the beads for the rosaries she made for the staff's Christmas presents.

That had been what she had been doing the day of the abduction—journeying to a market to buy beads and supplies for the rosaries that she and Gabriella were going to make that day.

An act of kindness that had gotten her killed.

"He never told me." There was a touch of hurt in Chance's words.

"He…" She took in another breath of fresh air. At least she wasn't trapped in the house, she told herself. At least she was on a horse. "He remembers more than I do. It is painful for us."

"Of course."

They fell into silence after that. Soon, she could see nothing but wilderness around her. The ribbon of trees she'd seen earlier was winding its way closer to the path they were on. The trees were trying to bud out. She could see the tips of the bare branches turning red with new growth.

Gabriella put thoughts of her mother out of her mind. It was not difficult—she'd had a great deal of practice. "We don't have winter in Mexico City. This is all so different here. Even the horses are different."

"Wait until they start shedding," Chance said with a chuckle. "The mess is something." They rode on in silence, then he said, "That hill over there? Nothing but bluebells in the spring."

"I would love to see them." Would they still be here in the spring, barricaded in Alejandro's house and hoping that *today* would be the day he remembered?

"If you're still here, you'll have to come back." He cleared his throat. "Do you know if you'll still be here?"

She shook her head. Was he asking because he was trying to pinpoint the best time to make another attempt—or was there something more genuine in his tone? "Alejandro does not want to return with us."

That still confused her, but now that she'd gotten out of the house and was riding across Texas, perhaps she could see why Alejandro wanted to stay.

"How is he today?"

"The same." Chance did not need to know that his name had caused a flash of recognition in Alejandro. Not yet, anyway.

They rode on, with Chance pointing out the features of the land and Gabriella trying to imagine how it would wear its spring coat. "Is it different than your ranch?" Chance asked.

They were still riding side by side, with Joaquin several feet behind them. For the first time in a great long while, Gabriella had the illusion of freedom. She was riding across land that was not surrounded by fences and patrolled by armed guards. No other signs of civilization crowded the view.

"Yes," she answered as the breeze played over her face. "We have far more trees. We do not have winter as a season—it does not get below freezing, except in very rare cases. Right now is a dry time." The ranch would be wearing its shades of brown. "I had hoped to see snow."

"We don't get a heckuva lot of snow," Chance replied. "Although when we do, it's real pretty. Makes the world look all new."

She looked at him as he rode. He sat tall in the saddle, one hand casually resting on his muscled thigh. He seemed perfectly at ease riding next to her. A true cowboy, she thought with a small smile.

He turned his head and caught the smile. "What?"

She could feel her cheeks flushing, so she quickly came up with a response to hide her embarrassment. "You said Alejandro would ride here with you?"

"Yup." Chance's gaze darkened. "He liked to race. Franny, my cook, would pack us a lunch and then we'd see who could make it to this shady spot down by the creek first."

It was obvious from his tone that the memory hurt him—not the pain of what had happened, though, but the pain of what he had lost.

Without thinking about it, she reached across the distance that separated them and touched his arm. "He will come back to us."

Chance met her gaze with nothing but challenge. "Which *he* is that? Your brother or my friend? Because I don't think that's the same man."

Then he looked back over his shoulder. Gabriella did the same. Joaquin was only a few feet behind them.

She sighed in frustration. Just the illusion of freedom. Not the real thing.

Five

Was she pulling his leg? Or was Gabriella del Toro being honest with him? And, more importantly, would Chance be able to tell the difference?

After all, he'd thought that Alex Santiago had always been an up-front kind of guy, and see where that had gotten him? The main suspect in Alex's kidnapping.

But Gabriella... She was something different. He didn't want to think that she'd been lying to him, not about her mother. The pain in her eyes had been all too real to be an act.

He was pretty sure. Recently he hadn't been the best judge of character.

He still couldn't get his head around what she'd said. He'd sort of understood the need for a bodyguard—after all, Alex had been kidnapped by someone, and if his family was as wealthy as they said they were, Chance could see why the del Toros would need twenty-four-hour protection.

But her mother being kidnapped when Gabriella was four—and killed? Her father keeping her under constant surveillance ever since—and occasionally scaring the hell out of her?

Chance had not particularly liked the man at their first meeting. Now? He had no idea how he was supposed to not punch the living daylights out of Rodrigo del Toro without getting shot. To put his daughter through attempted kidnappings—some of which had obviously terrified her—was right smack-dab between cruel and unusual.

He snuck a glance at Gabriella out of the corner of his eye as they rode down the path. She didn't look as though she was about to start sobbing, which was a small comfort. Chance prided himself on his honest dealings with the fairer sex, but crying women always made him nervous.

Her shoulders were back, her head up. Instead of jeans and cowboy boots, she was wearing a pair of buck-colored riding pants that fit her better than any glove ever could and English-style riding boots. She wore what appeared to be a sweater underneath a long jacket—not quite the barn-coat style he wore, but much more tailored to her shape.

Not that he was noticing her shape, but in that outfit, how could he not? She'd been stunning when he'd first seen her, but the long sweater-coat she'd had on had hidden some of the curves that were now highlighted. The woman had a hell of a body—the kind that made him want to slide his hands down her hips and hold on tight.

She was something different—not like women here. If a local woman had a body like that, she'd either be forever dieting to lose that elusive last ten pounds or dressed to maximize her assets—to use her body as a weapon.

Gabriella appeared to be neither of those things. Instead she looked stunningly regal, not cowered or afraid. Maybe that was because of the man behind them who probably had Chance in his sights. But maybe it was because she wasn't that bothered by the little story she'd told.

That thought depressed the hell out of him, but he wasn't exactly sure why.

Then she spoke. "Can I… Can I see the picnic spot?" Her voice quivered a bit, as if she was trying to master her feelings.

"You wanna race?" He didn't know what else to say. There was something bothering him about her little story— well, there was a hell of a lot that bothered him about it. But there was something that didn't add up.

She gave him a knowing smile. "I would love to, but I doubt that Beast would be able to keep up with your quarter horses and Joaquin will not appreciate being left behind."

Then he realized what it was—the bodyguard.

"Hey, if you're father's such a hard-ass—" She shot him a scolding look. "Pardon my French," he quickly added. "But if your father is so *concerned* with his family's safety, how come Alex didn't have a bodyguard up here? Aside from Mia, he lived alone. No armed thugs anywhere."

If anything, Gabriella blushed harder, which had the unfortunate side effect of making Chance forget what he'd asked. Truthfully, he couldn't remember a woman looking nearly as beautiful up on horseback as she did right now. Although she'd been a little skittish around Beast, she was perfectly at ease. Her long, lean legs gripped the saddle as if it was second nature to her.

Cara had never been as comfortable in the saddle as Gabriella was—and that was something that couldn't be faked. It would almost be worth getting plugged in the back just to watch her ride, hell-for-leather.

"As I'm sure you can appreciate, Mr. McDaniel—"

"Chance."

She turned to look at him, a warm smile on her face. "Chance."

The way she said his name—as though she was savoring a fine wine—made something clench low in his gut. In that moment he honestly didn't care if her brother was a habitual liar or her father was a sadistic control freak. He didn't much care if she was making up heart-wrenching stories to jerk him around. All he wanted to do was to see if she'd kiss him back, because he sure as hell wanted to kiss her.

"As I'm sure you can appreciate," she went on, a coy smile curving her full lips upward, "neither Alejandro nor I has always *enjoyed,* shall we say, the full protection our guards provide."

"Teenage rebellion?"

She nodded as the horses continued toward the picnic spot. "When Alejandro took a job at Del Toro Energy upon completing his studies, he moved to an apartment in Mexico City. He still had a guard, but he was allowed to come and go as he pleased. He went to clubs and events all over the city. He was very popular."

He heard a faint note of pain in her voice, one that said, loud and clear, that she had not been allowed to do any of those things. And just like that, Chance wanted to deck Rodrigo for keeping his daughter under what sounded like house arrest for her entire life. "He was popular here, too. A great guy." Or he had been, anyway.

She nodded in appreciation of that. "I am glad to hear it. When Papa wanted him to come north, Alejandro said he would not do it if he had to bring Carlos with him—that was his guard. He said Americans did not live like that."

He wanted to be known as an American, not a Mexican, Chance thought. Just part of the act.

"Of course," she mused, "he was still abducted, so I am not sure how sound his theory was."

"We're here," he said as a smaller trail branched off from the main path. Chance urged his horse forward to lead the way through the trees.

For every question Gabriella answered, he had another three. She had a good enough reason that Alex hadn't had a bodyguard in Texas—but why the hell had his father wanted him to come here in the first place? And why under an assumed name?

Had anything—the drinks at the club, the picnics by the creek—about Alex Santiago been real? Or had it all been part of some grand plan? Ruining his good name couldn't be it, although it sure felt personal on a bunch of different levels. But he'd never heard of Rodrigo del Toro before the man had showed up in Royal, causing a ruckus and bossing around the locals, so Chance didn't think that was it.

If it had all been fake, how much of what Gabriella said was trustworthy? Everything about her said genteel and proper—a noblewoman in the twenty-first century. She blushed easily but didn't lose her cool. She spoke of her life with a measure of reserve, without blatantly angling for sympathy.

Hell, he didn't know what to make of her.

So he stopped and dismounted near the creek. It was so low as to be nonexistent—not enough rain or snow this winter to balance out the last few years of drought that had savaged Texas. Chance sighed heavily. Trucking in water for his cattle wasn't cheap or easy, but if he didn't, he wouldn't have any animals for his dude ranch. People might still come for the rustic bunkhouse hotel or the trail rides—when the temperatures weren't over a hundred degrees, that was—but it wouldn't be as many.

Damn, but they needed rain.

"Need help?" he asked her, but before the words were out of his mouth, she was on the ground, loosening Gale's cinch and patting the horse on the neck. She grinned at him over Gale's neck. Right. She could handle herself.

So, feeling obligated, he turned to Joaquin. "How about you?" The big man on the big horse shook his head.

"He is fine," Gabriella translated. "He is better able to monitor the situation from horseback."

"Plus, no mounting block," Chance said, half to her and half to the guard.

"True." She said it, but Joaquin nodded in agreement.

He had to hand it to her—he could easily believe that Joaquin had been shadowing her for more than a decade. They had the kind of unspoken understanding that only came with years of constant contact. He found himself wondering how old Joaquin was. He had to be too old for Gabriella, didn't he? Surely Rodrigo del Toro wouldn't have tolerated his daughter being attracted to someone who was basically hired help?

The picnic spot was a small clearing on the edge of what used to be his creek. There was enough space for the horses to graze, but the trees stood tall here, blocking out the worst of the Texas heat in the summer.

"Have you lived here your whole life?" she asked as she walked around.

He wished he'd had Franny pack a lunch for them. He didn't want to take her back to the bunkhouse, to know that other ears were listening.

"Yup." He pointed to the low branch that reached across the creek bed. "See that rope burn? I used to swing into the water here. Over where that shallow puddle is? When the creek was full, that was my swimming hole—almost seven feet deep."

He picked up a rock and tossed it into the puddle. It made a depressingly small *plunk*. The creek hadn't been full in years. Man, he wished it would rain.

"Did you and Alejandro swim?"

Chance chuckled. "Nope. I think he waded in once." Then, because he couldn't help the vision that floated up in front of his eyes of Gabriella in some sort of swimsuit, he asked, "Do you swim?"

She didn't answer right away, instead, bending over and picking up a rock of her own. "We have a pool on our estate." She threw the rock, hitting the dead center of his swimming puddle.

"I put a pool in up at the bunkhouse when I opened

the hotel," he said, wondering if she'd have a one piece or a bikini—and how little that bikini might cover. Didn't matter—she'd fill it out. All of it. "We'll open it up in a few months."

The *if you're still here* hung out there, but now he wasn't sure that Gabriella—or Alex—would still be here. The more he learned about Rodrigo del Toro, the more he believed the older man would do anything to make sure his family was "secure."

She could easily be playing the poor-little-rich-girl card right now—held virtual prisoner by her mean father, never allowed to roam outside, never allowed to live a normal life. She could be trying to pluck at his heartstrings; make him feel as though he was her only possible savior from a life of house arrest.

She would be—if she was trying to manipulate him. He felt sure about that.

She turned to him, a sunny smile brightening her face. "When did you open the hotel?"

"A couple of years ago. I host theme weddings and week-long vacation packages. Hell—"

She shot him a look. "Heck," he corrected himself, "I even hosted a *Dallas*-themed murder mystery dinner when they launched the reboot on TV."

Nothing in her face changed—not on the surface, anyway, but it was like watching a shadow pass over her face. Everything about her got…colder. "The land is valuable to you?"

What the hell? He'd lost her—and he had no idea why. "It's been in my family for almost a hundred years—I'm the fourth generation of McDaniels to ranch here. There was no way I was going to let it go without a fight. Running a hotel and dude ranch may not be the same kind of hard work my grandpa did, but I do all right." Far better than his parents had done, that was for sure.

She gave him a measured look for another beat or two, then the shadow moved on and she was walking back over to Gale, tightening the cinch and swinging up into the saddle as though she'd been doing it all her life. She sure hadn't needed his help mounting up earlier and he felt a little stupid for having done so.

But he'd wanted to touch her, to see what she'd do. Would she have taken it as the come-on it sort of was—and would she have tried to use the attraction he obviously felt to her advantage?

She hadn't. She'd just looked down at him with that confused, almost innocent air about her. Which had done things to him.

Things that might get him shot by the end of the day.

He mounted up and they headed back down the trail toward the bunkhouse. "Franny will have lunch waiting on us," he said into the silence, although she had not questioned them returning the way they came.

"Tell me more about Alejandro here." The way she said it, it was less a conversation, more a cross-examination.

Yeah, this wasn't datelike activity. This was riding with the enemy—a woman who had access to the one man who could clear Chance's name in this whole mess. A man who apparently didn't remember a damn thing. A man who might be vulnerable to suggestion.

It didn't matter how attracted he was to Gabriella del Toro, how touching her stories were. Hell, it didn't matter a damn bit how well she rode. The only thing that mattered was clearing his name. A distant second to that was figuring out what had happened to his friend.

"What do you want to know?"

"You said he was popular here?"

"Yup. He rolled in and started throwing money around like it was confetti. A lot of people were suspicious, but money talks." Hell, he'd been one of the doubters—what had Alex Santiago known about Royal, Texas?

"Indeed." She didn't seem surprised by these statements. Then she turned her face toward his and broke out an absolutely stunning smile. "What is the phrase? All hat, no cows?"

The laugh burst out of him before he could think better of it. She giggled along with him, even as she looked mildly embarrassed. "Close, really close," he said, wiping an honest-to-God tear from his eye. Man, he hadn't laughed that hard since... Well, since before Alex had gone missing. "All hat, no cattle. But you've got the drift."

She gave him a funny look—funny confused, not funny amused. Although she still looked amused. "The what?"

"The drift. You understand the basic idea of all hat, no cattle." He looked at her. "Say, where'd you learn to speak English?"

Color rushed to her cheeks, which had him staring. "Am I not making myself clear?"

"No—it's not that at all." Jeez, he was sticking his foot in his mouth. "You've got a different accent. Not quite Mexican, but not American, either. It's real pretty," he added, although he didn't know why.

Well, he knew why. It was the same reason he shouldn't be complimenting her. Any attraction he felt for Gabriella del Toro was irrelevant. He had to remember that.

This was going to prove hard, what with her fluttering her thick black eyelashes at him and looking all pleased with his compliments. "Papa did not like the American accent. All of my tutors were British."

Chance was getting the feeling that dear ol' Papa didn't like anything American—which led to the inevitable question of why he had sent his son up here. "Alex's tutors— were they British, too?" Because Alex hadn't talked quite the way Gabriella had. He'd gotten the drift of all hat, no cattle from the get-go, no explanation needed.

At that, her cheeks flushed and she dropped her gaze away from his. *That'd be a no,* he thought. Then she answered the question. "Papa saw more value for Alejandro to be familiar with American slang."

Okay, so Rodrigo had raised his son to be a— What? A mole? Trained him to infiltrate the bustling urban hub of Royal, Texas?

And he held his daughter to a different set of standards— like a bird in a gilded cage.

Chance detested men like Rodrigo del Toro—men who used their family as pawns and, worse, who hid their manipulations behind the façade of concern and care. His own parents might not have had much of a go at running a successful ranch, but by God they'd loved him—and each other—and done everything they could to raise him up right.

This meant not saying the things that were running loose in his head right now, because it was clear that, no matter what he thought about the man, his daughter somehow managed to still love him. Instead he damn near bit his tongue trying to keep his mouth shut. It wasn't his place to judge what went on in other people's families. He wasn't about to start casting stones. Lord knew he had enough sin.

So he took the easy way out. "Well, if you need anything explained, you let me know."

"I will."

Funny, he thought as the barn came into view.

She sounded as if she meant it.

Six

They rode up to the barn and dismounted. "Where do the saddles go?" she asked as Marty came out to meet them.

Chance looked over and saw that she already had the saddle off the horse and was standing there as if he expected her to rub ol' Gale down herself. "Marty'll get it."

"I don't mind. I curry my horse at home."

Behind her, Joaquin nodded. He'd managed to stick the dismount and was also undoing Beast's cinch.

Gabriella may be coddled, but she wasn't spoiled. "Marty will get it," he repeated. A flash of defiance crossed her face, so he added, "Fran's got lunch waiting on us."

She looked as if she wanted to argue, but at the mention of lunch, everything changed. "Of course—I forgot. I groom Ixchel." She handed the saddle over to Marty, who looked bemused by a guest insisting on working.

They began the short walk up to the bunkhouse. "What does So-cheel mean?"

"Ixchel," she repeated, her lips smoothing out all the rough edges of the word. "She is the Mayan goddess of midwifery and, to a lesser extent, medicine."

"Sure." He'd never heard of her, but that didn't mean it was a weird name. But he wasn't going to say that.

Not that he needed to. She gave him a sly look and said, "Is it so much different than naming a horse after the founder of modern nursing—Florence Nightingale?"

He was probably gaping at her, but he couldn't help himself.

She laughed. That light, easy sound. "Although I am sure you had the songbird in mind, yes?"

"Yeah, that was what I was going for. Seem to have missed it by a country mile, though."

"Is that different than a city mile, then?"

"Sort of. Fewer sidewalks, more twists and turns. Have to go slower."

They reached the front doors of the Bunk House. He held the door for her, but Joaquin—who had trailed them the entire time—insisted that Chance go in second.

"Oh," Gabriella breathed in that slightly surprised voice as she looked around.

"It's not a real bunkhouse," he explained as she gaped at the three-story lobby, finished in rough-hewed logs and decorated with plush leather furniture and thick Navajo rugs. The decorator he'd hired had wanted to use deer antlers as accessories—for lamps and chandeliers and whatnot—as well as cowhides for rugs, but Chance had put his foot down. He didn't live *in* the bunkhouse, but it was still his home and he wasn't about to have the McDaniel name associated with clichés like that.

"The old bunkhouse was falling apart—Marty liked it, but he was the only one. So I had it leveled and I built this one."

She did a slow turn as she stared up at a three-tiered wrought-iron chandelier with mica shades before turning to face the massive stone hearth, the chimney running up the length of the wall. "I used Texas red sandstone—rough-cut—for the chimney and had the chandeliers custom-made by a guy I know."

"Amazing," she said as she did another slow turn. "You live here?"

"Nope. My house is a little farther out on the range. I grew up in that house."

"Oh, you live with your parents, as well?"

He wanted to be amused. If an American woman had asked that question, it would have been loaded with disgust that a grown man still lived with his momma. But for Gabriella, no such disgust existed. If anything, she sounded happy to have found a bit of common ground with him.

"They passed on. Back when I was in college. I'm the only McDaniel left."

Maybe he shouldn't have put it in exactly those terms, because Gabriella looked at him with her big, beautiful eyes—eyes that pooled with unshed tears. She reached out and laid her hand on his arm for the second time today. "Oh—my apologies. I didn't know."

More than anything, he wanted to touch her back—to put his hand on top of hers, to feel her skin underneath his.

Light flashed off of her neck and, for the first time, he noticed the jewelry she was wearing today. Whereas she'd had on ropes of turquoise in Alex's house, today she had on simple silver crosses.

He leaned in closer. Maybe not so simple. The surface of the cross at her neck was hammered, but the texture was so finely done that it looked solid from a distance. In the center was a green stone—small, but exquisitely cut. A perfect emerald.

She noticed him looking and tilted her head back, giving him full view of her smooth collarbone. He forgot about the necklace until she said, "The earrings match."

He dragged his gaze away from her chest and up to her ears. The crosses did indeed match—hammered silver with a small but perfectly cut emerald in the center. "They're stunning."

"Thank you." A soft pink blush flooded her cheeks—and edged down her collarbone.

Innocent, he thought. Sweet and innocent, with a hint of pride in her tone.

Unless it was all an act.

"Did you make them?"

"Yes. That is my business."

He knew he was probably staring at her with his mouth open like a catfish, but he couldn't help it. The work was amazing—not some mass-produced, made-in-China crap that any teenager could buy at a mall. "You make jewelry?"

"Yes." She removed one earring, then the other. Finally, moving at a speed that made something deep inside Chance hurt, she lifted her hair away from her neck and unfastened the necklace. She was still fully dressed, of course, but watching her remove her jewelry was one of the more erotic moments of Chance's life. Something about it felt intimate—forbidden, almost.

If he wasn't staring at her before, he sure as hell was now.

"There is a trick," she explained, taking a few steps over to the table in the center of the lobby. "The pieces are interlocking."

As he watched, her fingers nimbly arranged the three crosses. The interior arms of the two earring crosses slipped behind the top of the cross pendant, then she snapped the arms of the pendant behind the center of the smaller crosses. "It took me months to figure out how to balance the needed thickness to make them lock into place with the flexibility to bend but retain their shape." She demonstrated by picking the trio of crosses up and giving it a light shake. It didn't fall apart.

"You made that?"

"The three crosses," she said, a pleased smile on her face. "Tres Cruces—that is the name of my business." She put the assembled piece into his hand and then turned it over. "This is my mark."

She pointed to a small indent on the back of each separate piece—and damned if it wasn't three crosses lined up exactly as she'd arranged them on his table. Tres Cruces—tTt.

"I didn't realize you were so accomplished." Too late, he did realize that was a backhanded sort of compliment. "I mean, I didn't realize you did metalwork. Obviously, I realized you were quite accomplished—figured that out when you spoke such pretty French." She giggled at him and he felt foolish—but also pleased. "Yeah, I'll stop talking now. First rule of holes and all that."

Her eyes still brimming with good humor, she said, "The first rule of holes? What is that?"

"The first rule of holes—when you're in one, stop digging."

"Ah. An Americanism." She still looked a little confused. "What hole are you in that you must stop digging?"

Chance ran a hand through his hair. "Yeah—I'm embarrassing myself." But he had to admit it was sort of worth it to hear the lightness of her laughter. "Do me a favor and save me from myself—tell me about your business."

Just then, Carlotta, a receptionist at the front desk, hurried past him. "*Buenos días,* Señor McDaniel."

"*Buenos días,* Carlotta," he replied, handing Gabriella's three crosses back to her and forcing himself to take a step away. Not only was he running the risk of Joaquin plugging him in the back, but if Chance's staff saw him making googly eyes at a woman—well, word would get around.

He wasn't interested in one-night—or one-afternoon—stands. He didn't want to be the last McDaniel, but so far he hadn't done a bang-up job of finding a woman who'd cotton to his way of life. Cara Windsor sure hadn't, although he'd thought for a while she might be willing to give it a go. Before Alex Santiago had come and turned his whole life upside down.

"Carlotta, can you tell Fran we're here?"

Carlotta snuck a curious glance in at Gabriella before she said, *"Sí, señor."*

Chance watched her go, wondering how fast news of Gabriella's arrival would spread through his staff—and whether anyone would believe that he wasn't making the moves on Gabriella.

He sighed heavily. Just another sordid tale in the life of a fictional character named Chance McDaniel—first he kidnapped his best friend and dumped him south of the border, then he wined and dined his best friend's sister, no doubt corrupting her innocence. What next—he'd been plotting to overthrow the mayor? Conducting satanic rituals on his land? He was getting damn tired of people choosing to believe what they wanted about his life instead of what was true. He'd hoped things would get better now that Alex had been found, but with his memory gone, he hadn't exactly been able to prove that Chance had had nothing to do with his disappearance.

He forced himself back to the present, but it was tough. Gabriella spun his head around way too easily. "The restaurant is this way."

He led Gabriella and Joaquin off to the north side of the lobby, where an open doorway was framed with huge rough-cut logs. The restaurant wasn't a big thing—twenty tables—but it did a brisk business thanks to Franny's cooking.

Chance guided Gabriella—with Joaquin close behind them—to two tables in the corner of the restaurant. It was quiet today—they had a few people already here for the wedding tomorrow, but most of them were out doing wedding-related preparations for tomorrow.

Basically, they had the place to themselves.

"The tables are rather small," Gabriella noted, one of her delicately curved eyebrows lifting in what he hoped was amusement and not irritation.

"We like to promote a quiet atmosphere here, so, yeah—Joaquin, you'll be at this table here." Chance saw the look that the two exchanged, but he didn't care. Sure, Joaquin was probably a great guy, but Chance would like to get through a conversation with Gabriella without having the big man staring daggers at him. Besides, Gabriella seemed to be smiling. "You've got your back to a wall and full view of the room. Try not to shoot anyone, okay?"

Joaquin glared at him.

Franny came bustling out of the kitchen, wiping her hands on her apron. A big woman, Franny was in her mid-fifties, her children grown and living in Houston. She'd taken it upon herself to look after Chance. Some days, he could do without being henpecked, but most of the time, he appreciated that there was always someone on his side.

Franny not only didn't believe the rumors but would take a wooden spoon to anyone who dared repeat them in her presence. "It took you long enough," she began, wagging a finger at Chance as she scolded him. "'Bout thought I was going to have to eat the chicken all by myself." Then she rounded on Gabriella and all of her mother-hen attitude melted into a warm, broad smile that matched her warm, broad body. "Well, now—is this our Alex's sister?"

Gabriella glanced at Chance. He could tell this announcement made her uncomfortable, but he doubted that Franny had noticed the same thing. Instead, Gabriella said, "Hello. Yes, I'm, um, Alex's sister. Gabriella del Toro." She held out her hand.

But instead of shaking, Franny swallowed her up in a big old hug. Gabriella let out a little squeak.

"It's such a pleasure to meet you. We were so worried about Alex—why, that boy's practically family out here."

Fran finally released her grip on Gabriella to wipe a tear from her eye. "I was so afraid some drug cartel had gotten him or something—that violence slips a little farther north every year. And then, everyone tried to pin it on our Chance—all because of a woman! Well, I never." She clucked.

"Ah, yes," Gabriella said in a soft voice. "We do not believe it was a cartel."

Something in Chance hardened at her tone—and not the fun way, either. He'd never believed it'd been a cartel out for revenge—but then, he'd always believed that Alex had been a stand-up guy.

What did Gabriella believe? She had to have heard the rumors—maybe the law officers still investigating the case had mentioned him as a suspect. Did she believe them?

Damn that Alex Santiago—or Alejandro del Toro. Damn both of them. If he'd been up front from the get-go, none of this would have happened. If he could remember something—anything—Chance could get on with his life.

"And who is this fine specimen?" Franny had finally noticed Joaquin. "My, my!" She walked over to him and squeezed his bicep. "Hello there. I'm Fran."

Gabriella giggled as Joaquin blushed and blushed hard. It was, hands down, the biggest reaction Chance had seen anyone get out of the man. "It is a pleasure to meet you," he offered in a tentative voice.

"Now, you all sit yourselves down and let Franny get you some lunch." She winked at Chance as she ushered Gabriella over to the table with him. "Best fried chicken in the state!"

When she was gone, Gabriella turned to look at him. She kept on looking at him as he held out her chair for her and when he'd taken his seat across from her. Her gaze wasn't distrustful, not entirely—but it was clear that Franny had said something that she hadn't liked.

Here it comes, he thought.

But Gabriella waited until Franny had delivered salads and iced tea to both tables before speaking. "What did Franny mean, all because of a woman?"

He considered his position carefully before continuing. "Alex had a lady friend."

This was not the answer she was looking for. "Do you mean Cara Windsor, whose father owns Windsor Energy?"

Was that it? He'd been hearing the rumors—that Windsor Energy was the reason Alex had come to Royal in the first place. That would make sense, Chance figured. Maybe Rodrigo del Toro had wanted to check out his north-of-the-border competition. Industrial espionage.

Had industrial espionage been why Alex had taken Cara? The thought burned at the back of Chance's throat and Franny's sweet iced tea did nothing to cool him down. Cara had taken quite a shine to Alex—so much so that Chance had felt the only honorable thing to do was to step aside and let nature take its course. Had that all been a lie, too?

"I didn't have a damn thing to do with Alex's disappearance," he heard himself say.

"But you had been seeing this Cara Windsor." Gabriella's statement was quiet, as if she didn't want Joaquin to overhear her.

"We dated, but she was crazy for your brother. So I stepped aside. I cared for them both. Thought they'd be happy together." How stupid had he been? Had they all been?

Alejandro del Toro had been a mole from the very start. Chance had welcomed him into his life, onto his land— hell, into the Texas Cattleman's Club as a friend. He'd given up his girl in the name of honor and friendship. Not only had he been burned, but Cara had, too.

"You are angry." There wasn't much comfort in Gabriella's voice. Just an observation.

"You're damn straight I'm angry. I thought I had a friend, but it was an imaginary character named Alex Santiago. Then when he up and disappeared, everyone pointed their fingers at me, claiming I'd done it, maybe killed him because I was upset about Cara. Well, I am upset about Cara. I cared for her—enough to let her go—and it got us both burned. Maybe if I'd fought a little harder for her, he wouldn't have had the chance to screw her over like he screwed me over."

He immediately felt like a jerk—but hell, yeah, he was mad. He'd been watching his temper for far too long. Something had to give.

He waited. Gabriella would have something to say—but what? Denials? Defending her poor, injured brother? Accusing Chance of being as guilty as everyone said he was?

He wanted her to do just that—give him a good reason to hate her, to hate the entire del Toro family. Hell, he was worked up enough he wouldn't mind going a round or two with Joaquin—fists only, not guns. He was so damn tired of defending himself when he'd done nothing wrong. Not a single damn thing.

Franny came back out with plates of her fried chicken and Chance took the opportunity to dig in. Few things in this world were as good as Franny's fried chicken. Some people had encouraged her to open her own restaurant, but so far Chance had managed to hang on to her by taking care of the details—he provided the space and the staff and did the books, as well. All she had to do here was cook, which was fine by him.

"How you all doing?" she asked as she cleared the mostly uneaten salad plates. Her voice was light, but Chance could see that she was concerned.

He needed to stop grousing before he sent Gabriella

scurrying home with horror stories about how short-tempered he was. "Better now that your fried chicken's here."

"Go on, now," she said, gently swatting his arm before bustling back to flirt—yes, *flirt*—with Joaquin.

Gabriella watched her with amusement. "I do not think I have seen Joaquin blush that much in all our years together," she said in that quiet voice of hers.

He liked that quiet voice. He liked that she had things she wanted to say to him and only him. "Is that a bad thing?" Chance would never forgive himself if something bad happened to Franny.

"No, I do not believe it is," she said with a knowing wink.

Chance felt his mood improve. "So," he said, remembering where they'd left off before he'd lost his temper. "Tell me about Tres Cruces. Did you make that turquoise set you were wearing on Monday?"

She nodded. He could tell she was pleased that he remembered. "I was so very young when my mother died, you understand."

For a second Chance was afraid he'd asked the wrong question, but she went on without missing a beat. "I have so few memories of her, but one thing that has always stuck with me was that Mama liked to make rosaries for the staff for Christmas. She would let me pick out the beads and help me string them on the wire. When I dropped them—and I *always* dropped them—she would laugh and we would make a game out of who could collect the most beads the fastest." Her voice was softer, lighter—like a small girl lost in a happy thought. "I remember that clearly."

She smiled at the thought and he realized this was probably her most precious memory—and she'd shared it with him. It made him want to pull her into his arms and buy her more beads and take her on more rides—all so she could have a few more good memories. "So you learned from her?"

"In a way. It made me feel closer to her. I strung beads for a while, but soon I ran out of ideas and I wanted to try something new. Papa encouraged me, so there I was, this gap-toothed girl of ten, learning how to solder from one of the gardeners."

Chance whistled. "You were soldering at ten? I'm impressed."

"Alejandro used to tease me so," she said, her eyes lighting up. "My fingertips were always stained and I had little burns in much of my clothing. I was quite a sight in church on Sundays!"

They laughed, the tension of earlier gone. Maybe Chance would have to revise his opinion of Rodrigo del Toro—a little, anyway. Not too many fathers would let their daughters take up metalwork at an age when most girls were playing with dolls and painting their nails. "So you've been making jewelry for years?"

She shot him a sly look that made his blood pump faster. "Not all of it was a success, you understand."

"You should have seen the first fence I put up by myself. Not a straight line for a mile."

Something in her eyes...deepened. "A country mile?"

He grinned at her. She was a quick study—intelligent, beautiful *and* talented. Man, if things were different, he'd do a hell of a lot more than just take her out for a morning ride and then feed her fried chicken. Dinner with candles, a nice wine—maybe a long drive home on a slow country road? Too damn bad things weren't different. "Sure seemed longer when I was digging those post holes."

Behind him, he thought he heard Joaquin snort. Yeah, he forgot—they weren't exactly alone. What a pain in the backside. "So you make everything by hand?"

She nodded as she ate. "I have gallery shows in Mexico City. Most of my pieces are one-of-a-kind creations and I do a great deal of custom work. More than enough to keep me busy."

"Are you working here?"

"No," and the way she said it made it pretty clear that she missed it. "I was operating under the impression that we would not be in America long enough to pack up my tools and supplies." The more she talked, the sadder she looked. "I appear to have been mistaken."

Boy, no wonder she looked depressed. As far as he could tell, she spent her time riding her horse and making amazing jewelry. But at Alex's house? She had access to neither of those things.

"Any time you want to come out and ride," he offered, "you let me know. I'm hosting a wedding tomorrow, but I'll make time to hit the trail with you."

Her big eyes looked up at him with undisguised gratitude. "Thank you." Then she leaned forward. "I must admit, I was jealous of Alejandro coming to America, but this is the first time I've been able to get away from the house and see anything."

"I can show you around. For a town this size, there's a lot to do. We've got some good restaurants." He kept his voice level.

She didn't reply for a moment. Instead she looked at him through her thick lashes, her lips curved into the kind of smile that practically begged a man to come on over and kiss them. "Are you asking me out to dinner?"

The question felt like a trap because, yeah, he was asking her out to dinner. "I'm sure Alex would want to know that his little sister is enjoying herself in Texas—seeing the sights, that sort of thing. Not much point in coming to America if you're going to be stuck in a house."

He must not have done such a good job of covering his

tracks, because she shot him a look that was all kinds of hot and not a whole lot of innocent. "Joaquin will have to come along, of course."

"Of course." He tried to make it sound as if it was no big deal—just an armed chaperone. But if that was what it took to get her out of the house, then so be it.

Gabriella del Toro wasn't exactly a woman he could trust and, beyond that, she wasn't exactly in play, what with being a beautiful Mexican heiress with a domineering father and a lying, cheating dirtbag for a brother. She would only be here for as long as Alex couldn't remember who'd kidnapped him, then she'd be back south of the border again, locked up in her little castle and he'd never see her again.

But she'd unsaddled her horse. She soldered for fun. She spoke three languages.

And—this was the important part—she was sitting over there looking as if dinner was exactly what she had in mind.

"I think," she said, and he heard something new in her voice—soft, yes, but now it was mixed with what sounded like desire, "that dinner would be lovely."

Yeah, lovely.

Just like her.

Seven

When was the last time she'd had a date?

Gabriella mulled this question over on the drive back to Alejandro's house. Dating had been, by and large, a phase of life that she had skipped. She'd kissed a few grooms in the stable, but that had usually been retaliation against her father and his many rules. And they had never progressed past a few kisses—the grooms had been far more worried about being caught than Gabriella had been.

Then there had been her *quinceañera,* which had been a two-day-long festival her father had hired a party planner to orchestrate. Everything about her fifteenth birthday had been planned, including who her *chambelanes,* or dance partners, would be. Her father had chosen the son of one of his business partners, Raoul Viega, to be her first dance.

Ah, Raoul. That was probably as close as she could come to having dated. He was the same age as Alejandro and had attended the same university, although the two men had never been close friends. Raoul had been her escort at various points throughout the years, accompanying her to formal parties for Del Toro Energy and dinners at Los Pinos, the presidential estate.

She had kissed Raoul, of course. Occasionally because she had wanted to, often because he had kissed her first—

but mostly because she'd felt that each kiss was a small act of rebellion. A dare to Joaquin to report her activities back to her father, as he had always done about everything else.

To his credit, Joaquin had never related her "dates" to her father in the exact way that they happened. But Raoul had grown bored with simple kisses and Joaquin's presence had not allowed anything more…exciting to occur. Soon, Raoul had only taken her out when polite society dictated it, and those events had grown further and further apart. She had last seen him at her most recent gallery opening, eight months ago—and he'd accompanied a beautiful blond woman to the event.

Gabriella had gone with her father.

She'd been so miserable. Alejandro was in Texas—with no guards, no surveillance—and she had been stuck at Las Cruces, going places with Joaquin and her father. She knew she had no right to complain—she had never been cold or hungry, never been treated as chattel—but she'd still fallen into a deep depression after that. She didn't want to retreat further into herself—further away from the rest of the world. She'd wanted more than that.

She didn't want it on her father's terms, no matter how well-meaning those terms were.

Which is how she'd wound up in Texas, having lunch with Chance McDaniel. On her terms.

Raoul had always resented Joaquin's necessary presence, making rude comments about her guard when he could clearly hear them. Perhaps that was why Joaquin had never allowed Raoul and Gabriella to be alone long enough for anything else to happen besides those quick kisses.

But Chance? Well, that was different. It was quite clear that Chance was not exactly enamored with Joaquin accompanying her on the ride, but he had done an admirable job of including Joaquin.

Gabriella looked at Joaquin. He was tapping his fingertips on the steering wheel as he navigated the vehicle back to Alejandro's house. She leaned forward and caught the sound of humming—faint, but unmistakable.

She smiled with joy. He may never say it out loud—and certainly not in so many words—but Joaquin had enjoyed himself today, as well. What had been his favorite part—the ride or the meal? Or had it been the cook, Franny?

Excellent. If Joaquin had had a nice time and Gabriella's safety had never been in question—which, despite a rather strong set of hugs from Franny, it hadn't—then there could be no good reason not to return to McDaniel's Acres for another ride.

For the first time since she'd arrived in Texas, happiness flooded Gabriella. This was why she'd come, after all—to get off the estate, to see something new. To taste the freedom that Alejandro had enjoyed for two years.

Lost in this pleased state, they arrived back at the house and Joaquin escorted her inside. At first she didn't notice anything amiss, but then she heard it—a deep male voice that sounded as if the speaker hadn't talked for years, coming from the kitchen.

She rushed past Joaquin to find Alejandro sitting at the kitchen table. He'd showered and shaved since the morning, and had dressed in a white button-up shirt and clean jeans. He was drinking a cup of coffee and talking to Maria, the housekeeper, as if this were a normal Friday. When she entered the room, he looked up and smiled at her.

As though he knew who she was.

"Alejandro!" But that was all she could say as she threw herself at him. Her throat closed up and she was suddenly crying. He was back, the brother she remembered—not the stranger who'd come home from the hospital.

Wasn't he? As she clung to his neck, she waited for some sign from him that he did, in fact, remember her beyond the nice lady who brought him breakfast. For a moment nothing happened and she lost all hope. Nothing had changed, except he'd left his room. That was it.

But then he said, "Hi, sis," and hugged her back. "I've missed you."

"You know me?" she demanded, trying to keep herself composed. But then he leaned back and looked her in the eyes and she saw him. Her brother.

"I couldn't forget my little sister."

She almost cried. Alejandro was *here*. "I have been so worried about you," she said as she hugged him again. "You must tell me what you remember." Then, before she could stop herself, she added, "You must tell me if Chance McDaniel had anything to do with it."

A shade crossed over his face and she felt him slipping away from her. As if he was pretending.

She recalled that morning, when Chance's name had sparked some recognition in Alejandro's eyes. She'd thought he didn't trust her with whatever the truth was—but now?

What if it wasn't that he didn't trust her, but that he didn't trust Chance? Was Alejandro still afraid of his former friend?

But then he said, "Did you go for a ride?"

"Yes." The wash of confusion she felt right now did nothing to help her nerves. She disentangled herself from him and took a seat across the table.

"Oh, did you ride with Chance? He leads trail ride groups all the time," Maria said as she set a cup of strong coffee down in front of Gabriella.

"Thank you so much," Gabriella replied. Up until now, Maria had practically been her best friend here in Texas, the one woman she could talk to.

But right now, she had a great deal to discuss with her

brother and she'd like that conversation to be as far from prying ears as possible.

"I was filling Alex in on some stuff," Maria went on, wiping down the countertop as she spoke. Then, in the distance, the dryer buzzed. "Laundry!"

And they were alone. Well, Joaquin was still there, but it was essentially the same thing. Gabriella had so many things she wanted to ask Alejandro, but she didn't want to overload him and she also didn't want him to shut down on her again. So she sipped her coffee before asking, "Have you talked to Papa yet?"

"No," he said, not meeting her gaze. "He is in a meeting, I think."

She heard the disappointment in his voice. He'd finally decided to come down—and no matter what he said, she believed it was a conscious decision—and Papa hadn't taken the time to greet him.

"He has been very worried about you," she explained. It felt hollow. "We all have."

"I...didn't want you to worry." Again, he sounded as though he was measuring his words, testing the waters on how much information he could reveal. "I'm glad you are here."

Perhaps he was not comfortable with Joaquin? Of course Alejandro knew Joaquin was a trusted part of the security detail, but then, it had been years since the two men had spent a great deal of time in each other's company. Joaquin had become her guard when Alejandro was preparing to go to university.

"Joaquin, please tell Papa that Alejandro is feeling better."

No one moved for what felt like a very long time. If anything, Alejandro looked pleased with her directive, but he was careful not to actually smile. For his part, Joaquin seemed torn on what he should actually do. He was her guard, but his first duty had always been to Rodrigo del Toro. No doubt he was weighing fetching his boss versus listening to Gabriella and Alejandro's conversation.

"Please," Gabriella said with more insistence. "Papa will want to know that Alejandro is up."

Finally, Joaquin acknowledged her with a nod of his head and left the room. Gabriella and Alejandro sat for a moment longer, but she wasn't about to waste this precious time with him. "Tell me what you remember."

"Not much," he admitted, scrubbing a hand over his chin again.

"You know who I am?"

"My sister. Gabriella."

"Do you know who Joaquin is? Do you remember Papa?"

"Yes." He answered without hesitation, his gaze never leaving hers.

"Do you know our business?"

"Del Toro Energy."

He had to have been faking it this morning. Heavens, he had to have been faking it for some time. But how long? Had he had his memory back the whole time?

"Do you remember Chance McDaniel?"

At this, Alejandro blinked. He clasped his hands in front of him and stared at his thumbs. "Not really," he mumbled. But she could hear the untruth in his voice.

"What about Cara Windsor? Of Windsor Energy?"

Everything about him froze, answering the question in a way that words never could.

"Because I have heard rumors," Gabriella went on, pressing her advantage, "that you stole this Cara Windsor from Chance and that is why he took you and dumped you back in Mexico—it was revenge. Is that what happened?"

But before he could answer, Papa burst into the kitchen, followed closely by Joaquin. "Alejandro!" Papa bellowed.

Then he swept his son into his arms and patted him on the back with such force that Alejandro turned red in the face. "We must call the doctors and the police," Papa said. "We will find the people who did this to you and I will make them pay."

Alejandro shot a worried look at Gabriella. Yes, he had answered her questions. But he clearly did not want to answer more questions—questions with a bigger audience.

"Papa," she said, putting a hand on his arm. "Alejandro has just started to feel like himself. Perhaps it would be best to let him rest up for a few more days before we allow the authorities to question him. We do not want to risk making things worse."

Alejandro shot her a grateful look as Papa restrained himself. "Yes, yes, of course. Come, son, sit down. Have some coffee."

Then Maria bustled back in and the kitchen was filled with the sounds of talking and cooking as Papa and Maria both tried to encourage Alejandro to share more of what he remembered. But, for the most part, he said little more than "No, not really" or "I'm not sure" while he stared at his hands.

It was only after Maria had left—with enough dinners in the refrigerator so that Gabriella would not have to attempt cooking for another week—and Papa had taken another call from his office that she had the chance to ask the question that had burned in her mind the entire afternoon.

"Alejandro," she said, careful to keep her voice light. Joaquin was still in the room, after all. True, he was scrolling on his tablet, but they both knew he was listening. "I know you do not recall very much, but I had a nice ride today with Chance McDaniel. He showed me a place where you would picnic."

He made a face that reminded her of the one time Alejandro had caught her kissing one of the grooms. She had been fourteen.

Was that what this was now? Obviously, Alejandro had his secrets and would go so far to protect them as to lock himself in his room for weeks on end. As of yet, she did not have any secrets to speak of—except for the fact that she was sure her trip to McDaniel Acres had been less about proving Chance's guilt and more about Chance.

Yes, it was quite clear that Alejandro remembered the picnic spot—and did not necessarily approve of Chance taking her there. Just as he had not approved of her lowering herself to the level of kissing the hired help. "Chance has asked to escort me on other rides and to dinner. With Joaquin accompanying us, of course."

"Is that so," he said in that thoughtful voice, the one he'd used that morning. At least this time he hadn't said, "Who?"

He hadn't forbidden her to do those things—not a hint of worry at her being in the company of Chance McDaniel. Just…thoughtfulness. "Yes. So until you can remember anything about Chance McDaniel in connection with your abduction, I shall continue to do so. This is a good opportunity to investigate if he had any true motivations for wanting to harm you, after all."

Alejandro was shaking his head again—a small gesture, but one that made it clear that he didn't agree with this particular part of the plan.

She could hear Papa shouting in the distance. It sounded as if his business call had not gone according to plan and Gabriella doubted if she would get another quiet moment to speak with her brother for the rest of the day.

She stood and, under the pretense of gathering up Alejandro's cup to refill it, whispered, "Your secrets are safe with me."

He gave a curt nod with his head and then Papa was

back in the room, shouting about a deal that was on the verge of collapse.

Gabriella would keep her promise. If she kept the secret that Alejandro had been feeling better for some time... Well, then he would be in her debt. And that was not a bad place to have one's older brother.

But that didn't mean she wouldn't find out a little bit more.

Including whether or not Chance McDaniel would resort to violence to win Cara Windsor back.

Eight

Chance watched as the big black SUV pulled up along the paddock. The wedding was over and, being a Monday afternoon, his hotel was remarkably empty. This was as close to free time as he got.

And he was spending it with Gabriella del Toro.

He was *not* excited about her coming back out to the ranch. As far as he knew, she was being sent out here by that overbearing father of hers to look for "evidence" of his guilt or something ridiculous.

That didn't explain why he was looking forward to another ride. Maybe today, they'd get to race a little. Then they'd have dinner. He hadn't wanted to push his luck, so they'd still be eating Franny's home cooking. She'd saved him a couple of nice steaks with nothing more than, "Sure seems like a sweetheart," as an editorial comment.

Then Joaquin opened the back door and Gabriella's long legs slid out of the car. He saw today that instead of her riding jodhpurs and British-style boots, she had on a pair of sleek gray cowboy boots, a pair of dark jeans that fit her better than any pair of gloves ever could with a black belt at the waist and a light-colored denim shirt. God help him, she pulled a straw hat out of the backseat and settled it onto her black hair, once again pulled into a low braid. She was wearing her three crosses again, but that was it.

She'd been more of a princess the last time he'd seen her—both times, actually. But today? She was a cowgirl. She stepped around her guard and spotted him inside the barn door. Even at fifty feet, give or take, the sunlight shone off of her wide smile.

Oh, man—he was in trouble. What had been beautiful and refined before was now a little rougher looking, a little more ready to race.

A lot more ready to ride.

"Couldn't stay away, huh?" He couldn't help himself.

"I know Gale missed me—and my carrots," she replied as she headed toward him, her long legs closing the distance between them faster than he would have liked. The woman moved with a grace that he wanted to be sure to appreciate properly and he figured he was less likely to get blindsided by Joaquin if he was staring from a safe distance.

"I don't have her saddled yet." This had been on purpose. Part of her story hinged on being this great horsewoman. He wanted to see exactly how well she did with old Gale. "Beast is ready to go," he added to Joaquin. No need to push his luck with the big man.

She arched a manicured eyebrow at him, accepting his challenge. "Come on," he said, nodding his head in Gale's direction.

Gabriella walked beside him, her hand close enough to touch. Maybe he was imagining things, but he swore he could feel the warmth of her fingers as they swung past his hand. But Joaquin was about five feet behind them, so Chance kept his hands to himself.

He led her into the barn to where Gale was tethered in the middle of the aisle, her saddle waiting on the stall door. A bucket with a curry comb inside it was on the floor.

Maybe this wasn't a fair test—maybe she only rode in English saddles back home. But before he could tell her he'd do it, she had the comb in hand and was brushing down Gale's back, murmuring in Spanish the whole time.

Her English accent may be British, but damned if her Spanish wasn't pure poetry. Grooming a horse had never sounded so...sultry.

She settled the saddle blanket onto Gale's back. Then, exactly like a woman who knew what she was doing, she looped the stirrup over the horn of the saddle and set—not plopped—the saddle onto Gale's back.

A novice would have thrown the saddle up there, which made even the mellowest animal skitter around. But Gabriella had done everything perfectly.

As he watched, her fingers nimbly tightened the cinch strap and then she unhooked Gale from the tethers. When she turned to face Chance, the smile on her face was nothing short of victorious. She'd known exactly what he was about and more than exceeded his expectations.

What could he expect from her in bed? Her fingers moving with ease over his skin, her body responding to his every challenge?

Behind him, Joaquin cleared his throat.

Man, this was getting to be a problem.

Gabriella didn't seem concerned by the big man with the gun. Instead she only had eyes for him. "What would you like to show me today, Chance?"

Yes! a primitive part of his brain crowed in victory. His name on her lips had an immediate—and slightly awkward—effect on him. He went hard. Fast.

Luckily, between the jeans, the chaps and his buckle, there was little chance that anyone would notice his discomfort. Because that's what it was about to be, as she led Gale past him and he followed, eyeing his horse. Discomfort was mounting up with an erection. It bordered on hazardous to his health.

"I have a surprise for you," he replied, watching her hips sway as she walked out into the sunshine.

She paused and he felt Joaquin bristle. Oh, hell. Yeah, she probably didn't consider surprises a good thing. So he added, "A different part of the ranch—the part that tourists don't see. I want you to meet Slim."

Her cautious smile came back. "Slim? Is that a man or an animal?"

"He's a man," Chance replied, taking hold of her reins so she could mount up. "He's what we here in Texas call 'a crusty ol' fart.'"

She swung up into the saddle without a problem and he was forced to watch her bottom—full and round and barely contained by the jeans she wore—settle into the saddle. All he wanted to do was to run his fingers over that bottom and feel the fullness fill his hands.

This line of thinking did nothing to relieve his current condition.

Gabriella laughed again, her soft voice filling his ears. Man, he was in *so* much trouble. "I'm not entirely sure I understood that. Perhaps you should show me?"

Oh, he had things he wanted to show her, all right. But there were a few problems with that—problems that were bigger than Joaquin, who'd managed to heave his mass up onto Beast.

Problems such as Alex's missing memory. And half the town still thinking Chance had tried to do Alex in over a woman. And their father hating his ever-loving guts.

Beyond that, he had bigger problems. Maybe Alex would miraculously recover and Chance's name would be cleared and he could go back to being Chance McDaniel instead of the fictional character that looked just like him.

He had a terrible feeling that Alex might not be too

thrilled to know that Chance was having less-than-pure thoughts about his little sister.

Gabriella spun Gale in a neat circle so that she could look at him. Her eyes glowed with a warmth he hadn't seen in a woman's gaze in a long time. "Shall we?"

Was there any way to win here?

Nope.

"By all means, we shall."

He knew one thing. This whole mess might blow up in his face at any second.

But he wasn't going to quit trying.

Gabriella rode next to Chance. She couldn't keep the smile off her face, and she knew it. The breeze today held a hint of spring that made everything look greener.

Including his eyes. She couldn't help but meet Chance's gaze as he pointed things out. They took a different path this time, one that lead far away from the well-worn trail they'd taken to the picnic spot last time. But instead of growing more narrow or showing other signs of disuse, the path widened, tire treads clearly visible in the hardened dirt.

So wherever he was taking her wasn't some secret hidden away from the rest of the world. That was good.

Because when he'd said their destination was a surprise today, she'd been more than a little shocked that Joaquin hadn't hustled her back into the car at once. Taking her someplace where no one would think to look for them— or hear a struggle, much less gunshots—would be unacceptable.

But unless they changed course soon, it was clear that they were going someplace that was easily accessible and widely traveled.

"How is Alex today?"

The question seemed innocent—and sincere—but Gabriella hesitated. Papa had insisted that no one outside of the family know about Alejandro's recovery. He was afraid that if people knew Alejandro was starting to remember, his attackers would make another attempt. "Not much has changed," she lied, feeling horrid about doing so.

Chance seemed to take her at her word. Instead of pressing her further, he continued to point out features of his ranch.

"And over there," he said, pointing at a neat two-story house with a wide porch, "is my place."

"Lovely," she said. It was a bright yellow with green shutters. Empty flower planters hung under the windows. What did it look like on the inside? Back at Las Cruces, they had public rooms in the front where Papa took visitors. Those parlors were kept in a state of high shine in anticipation of impressing visitors.

But the rest of the house was far more comfortable. These had been the rooms that Gabriella had grown up in—the kitchen where she'd eaten her meals, the library where she'd taken her lessons with the other children on the estate—and her room. Those were the rooms she missed now.

Was Chance the same? Was the bunkhouse, as he called his motel, his public parlor? What did his private rooms look like? "Do I get a tour?"

Chance shot her a look she couldn't quite read. Was he pleased she'd showed an interest? Or was there something more to it? "Not today. I usually have one of the hotel maids come down every other week. It's kind of a mess right now." Then he leaned toward her. "Besides, not sure your man there would think that was a good idea."

Gabriella felt herself sigh. Chance was correct. No matter how she tried to dress it up as part of her investigation into Alejandro's abduction, seeing where Chance McDan-

iel lived had nothing to do with her brother and everything
to do with the man riding next to her.

At least he hadn't said no. Just not today. That implied
that he might very well show her his home at a later time.

Because he anticipated more rides.

They rode past the sunny house and on to a series of
sheds and buildings, all made of corrugated metal. "What's
this?"

"The shop area." He rode up to the first building and
dismounted, tying his horse to a post. "Here, let me help
you."

She tensed, almost expecting him to lift her out of the
saddle and definitely wishing he would. She would love
to feel his callused hands settle around her waist—would
love to feel them on her skin.

But he didn't. Perhaps ever-mindful of Joaquin, he took
the reins and held Gale still while Gabriella dismounted.
Then he kept a respectable distance between them as he
led her into the first building. "Here's where we keep the
mowers and ATVs—we use this stuff every day around
here," he said, his voice echoing off the metal walls.

"How...nice," she replied, not knowing what else she
was supposed to say.

They walked to the next building. "The bigger trac-
tors and implements are in here. We rotate planting cover
crops and alfalfa in the fields. Over there's my baler," he
said, pointing to a large, square machine.

"Lovely." As lovely as one could consider a baler. Whatever that was.

They walked past the baler and through a door at the
back of the building. Joaquin kept close, no doubt worried
about an ambush.

They entered what was clearly a workroom, the sounds
of grinding metal filling the air. "Hey, Slim!" Chance

yelled loudly, but the grinding didn't let up. "Be right back," he said to them as he headed toward the noise.

Gabriella looked around. *What a workroom,* she thought in awe. Pegboards lined the walls with such a variety of tools as she had never seen—and that was saying something. She had a well-appointed workroom back on the estate in an outbuilding, but this was something on an entirely different scale. Clamps, pliers, screwdrivers and so much more hung from the pegboards in descending order. She had smaller tools, but some of those clamps were designed to hold posts together, it appeared.

And those were just the tools on the walls. In her shop, she had a kiln and a small, portable furnace to melt her metal, grinders and other tools to shape the stones. Here, there were planers, lathes, saws and all manner of woodworking tools. Then, in the back, she spied a furnace—an honest-to-goodness furnace, the kind used to fire iron.

Suddenly the grinding stopped and she heard an older male voice say, "Eh? Oh, Chance, my boy!"

Then an older man that matched the voice came into view, a visor pushed back on his head, a dirty kerchief tied at his neck and a worn apron covering up his clothes. His steel-toed boots were so old that the steel was no longer covered by leather. He was patting Chance on the shoulder with a massive gloved hand.

"Brought someone to meet you," Chance was saying. He turned to Gabriella. "Gabriella, this is Daryl Slocum—also known as Slim."

Although he was probably well into his sixties—it was difficult to tell with the gear he had on—Slim rolled his eyes. "Never did cotton to the name Daryl."

What did "cotton" mean? Besides a plant they made fabric from.

"Slim," Chance went on before she could figure it out, "over there is Joaquin and this is Gabriella del Toro." Slim gave her a sideways glance, which made Chance add, "Alex's sister."

As realization dawned in Slim's eyes, Gabriella felt uncharacteristically frustrated. Of course she was "Alex's" sister—but she hated that being the thing everyone knew her by. She was always Alejandro's sister or Rodrigo's daughter. It was only when it came to her jewelry—her art—that she was Gabriella. That was how she preferred it.

Slim nodded—actually, it was almost a bow. "Well, howdy do, ma'am. A pleasure." But Slim made no move to shake her hand or—thankfully—hug her as Franny had done. "We sure were glad when they found Alex. I've been praying for him."

The sentiment caught her off guard. "Why, thank you. He is a little better."

At this, Chance gave her a quizzical look—one so brief she wasn't sure she'd actually seen it. Then he was talking again. "Slim made the chandeliers in the bunkhouse."

"You did? Those were beautiful!"

Slim blushed a deep maroon. "Shucks, it weren't nothin'. Just testing out a few designs. And I bought the shades." He said this last bit as if it made the ironwork little better than a pile of metal.

"They were perfect for the space. Simply amazing." She was being honest, too.

"Gabriella here is an artist." Chance motioned her closer. "Show him your stuff."

She frowned at Chance for the "stuff," but she removed her jewelry and pieced it together for Slim.

"I'll be dipped—you made that?" Slim whistled long and low when she nodded, pleased with the compliment.

At least, she assumed it was a compliment. She wasn't sure what "dipped" meant in this context.

"Gabriella's going to be staying on in Royal for a bit longer," Chance explained as Slim tried his hand at assembling the three crosses. "I thought she might need to borrow some tools."

What? Had he said—borrow *tools?*

Slim grinned. "Sure. Lemme show you what I got—no gold or silver, but I got a little bit of everything."

Even though Gabriella followed Slim, she couldn't absorb what he was showing her. All she could do was stare at Chance.

He was providing her with tools—the very things she hadn't taken the time to pack. Working on her jewelry and riding were the two things she'd missed most about Las Cruces—and Chance McDaniel was single-handedly giving her both. Without her having to ask. He just did it.

She thought Slim was showing her industrial-size spools of wire, but all she saw was Chance. Then his gaze met hers and she was filled with that unexpected sense of coming home. The emotion was so strong that her legs felt a little weak.

Of course Papa and Alejandro took care of her, but their definition of "taking care of her" was usually more limited to what was too unsafe for her to do—show her horses, attend university, date. To do anything outside of the patrolled walls of Las Cruces. Taking care of her was locking her up tight and giving her just enough to do to make her forget about being a prisoner in her own home.

Chance? He showed her around. He introduced her to people who obviously cared for him. He didn't keep himself separate from the staff the way Papa did. Instead he acted as if they were his family, and they the same.

Perhaps she was being foolish. This was probably nothing more than Chance had done for Alejandro, after all—welcomed him onto his land and into his life. Perhaps this was the sort of man Chance McDaniel was—friend to one and all.

But when Slim led them back through a row, Chance

put his hand on her. It was a light touch—one that started at her shoulder, one that probably signaled nothing more than a polite "you go first." But when she did, his hand did not leave her.

Instead his fingertips floated over her shoulder and down her back, ending above her bottom before they moved sideways. Then, briefly, he rested his hand on her waist.

The touch was unlike anything she'd ever felt before. Luiz, the stable boy, had touched her with fumbling, unsure hands. Raoul, her frequent escort to public events, had always taken hold of her arm as if he already owned her. There had never been a moment in which he'd asked for permission—not from her. Her father had given Raoul permission to accompany her and that was all the permission he needed.

But Chance's touch? It was something soft and gentle—confident but unassuming. His hand lingered at her waist for a moment longer, then they were through the narrow row and, with a final gentle squeeze, he withdrew.

"I do a lot of wrought iron," Slim was saying, but Gabriella found herself turning back to look at Chance.

"You okay?" he asked in a tone of voice that felt every bit as confident as his hand had.

"I…" She cleared her throat, thankful that Slim was now demonstrating his bellows. "I am surprised, that is all."

One of his eyebrows moved up, making him look playful. "A good surprise?"

"One of the best I have ever had." She wanted to do something completely rash, like throw her arms around his neck and show him exactly what she thought of his surprise—but then a blast of heat from Slim's furnace hit her.

"Any time you want to come out, you just give me a call. Slim here has been working on the ranch for close to fifty years. He's got every tool known to mankind. Never throws anything away."

Then—in full view of both Slim and Joaquin—he reached over and ran his hand down the length of her arm, lightly squeezing before he withdrew and took a step away from her.

Not a touch of ownership. A question. Asking permission.

Suddenly she wanted to say *yes* in a way she'd never wanted to before.

She glanced at Joaquin. The scowl on his face was more than enough to remind her that saying *yes* to Chance— heavens, just saying *thank you* in the way she wanted to— would be a challenge. How would she convince him to join her here on a regular basis? Working in the shop had nothing to do with investigating the ranch in regard to Alejandro's disappearance.

"So," Slim said, seemingly unaware of the unspoken battle she was waging with herself. "Whaddya think?"

"I have never worked in iron." She did not want to refuse Chance's gifts and it had nothing to do with not wanting to insult his honor. It had everything to do with the gratitude that filled her as she looked around the shop.

She could ride. She could work—not as she normally did, but it would be a new skill all the same. And—most importantly—she could be free of the confines of Alejandro's house.

She could be here. With Chance.

"Heck fire, I'll teach you! We'll start with the basics and then you can try your hand at some smaller pieces. I got some extra aprons—not sure if I've got one big enough for your husband there," he added as an afterthought.

"Joaquin is not my husband. He is my guard."

"Oh—right, my bad. I bet you all are a little jumpy

after what happened to our Alex. Sure, bring him along. Franny'll feed him if he helps out!"

At this, Joaquin's face turned a brighter shade of red, although nothing else about him changed. The others might not have noticed his blush, but Gabriella did.

Maybe, Gabriella thought with a new hopefulness rising up in her, it would not be so very difficult to convince Joaquin to return to the ranch on a more regular basis after all.

She looked at Chance and smiled. "My door is always open," he said, and she knew he was trying to sound as if this open invitation was the sort he would make to any visitor to his ranch.

But that's not what she heard. Instead she heard an unspoken *to you* in there—"My door is always open to you."

Then he added, "All you have to do is ask, Gabriella. The answer will be yes."

Yes.

The answer would be *yes.*

Nine

The look on Gabriella's face was something to behold.

As they said their goodbyes to Slim and headed back to where the horses were tethered, she kept those big beautiful eyes latched on to him with the kind of look that made him wish he was in a honky-tonk and it was Friday night.

When they made it back to the horses, she turned to him. "You did this for me?"

"Yup." Out of the corner of his eye, he saw Joaquin take hold of Beast's reins. He wasn't making any sudden moves toward his weapon.

Gabriella didn't seem concerned about whatever Joaquin may or may not be doing. She only had eyes for him.

Which had been the point.

She took a step closer to him. The space between them was only a couple of feet, but it sure felt a lot less than that. He could almost reach out and touch her again.

He did no such thing.

But God help him, he wanted to—and not as if he was afraid of who might be watching. He wanted to pull her into his arms and take the kiss that she sure looked as though she wanted to give him.

"This is the most thoughtful thing anyone has ever done for me." Her voice was soft. Warm.

Inviting.

He stood rooted to the spot because if he moved, he knew he'd take what she was offering and he also knew that he'd get shot and he really wished he didn't know both of those things at the same time. "Welcome," he managed to say without pulling her into his chest.

She shot him a look that took everything soft and sweet about her and turned it hard and needy in a heartbeat. "I would like for you to put your hands in your pockets."

If anyone else had asked him to do that, Chance would have known they were planning on punching him and he'd have had none of it. But Gabriella wasn't going to crack him across the cheek because of Slim, was she?

The light in her eyes said no. Hell, everything about her said no.

So he did.

Her gaze flicked back to where Chance was pretty sure Joaquin was still watching them. He could only hope the barrel of a gun wasn't pointed at the back of his skull. "As you can see, he is not touching me," she said in an all-too-businesslike voice.

Then, before he could make any sense of that, she stepped toward him, flung her arms around his neck and kissed the holy hell out of him. Her teeth clipped his lower lip and he desperately wanted to tilt his head to the side so that he could taste her better—taste all of her—but he couldn't move. He didn't dare.

When it ended—and damn it, it did end—she pulled away so quickly she almost stumbled. And he almost got his hands jerked out of his pockets to grab her.

She regained her footing and took that all-important step away from him. "You see? He did not touch me."

She wasn't talking to him. She was talking to Joaquin. It was almost as if she had something to prove and he was it.

"I want to race back to the barn," she announced, her color high and her eyes bright. "Straight back."

He knew she was asking her guard—not him—but he answered anyway. He barely managed to avoid saying *darlin'* but somehow he kept that part in his head only. "All you had to do was ask. You knew the answer would be yes."

Man, that smile—her wanting to race—that *kiss*.

They mounted up and took off, hell-for-leather. He could hear Gabriella's laughter over the pounding of the horses' hooves—even over the sound of Joaquin cussing in an interesting mixture of English and Spanish.

Was he a greedy bastard? Maybe. Maybe that's exactly why he reined Ranger in a bit, why he let Gale pull ahead. He couldn't touch her—even she admitted as much with her request to put his hands in his pockets.

But he sure as hell was going to watch her ride.

Her backside fit into that saddle as though he'd had it custom-made for her. She rode low against Gale's neck, no doubt urging the horse on faster. He had a hell of a view.

She liked to ride. Hell, she *loved* to ride. She was interested in stuff like wrought iron. She saddled her horse. He'd be willing to bet a steak dinner she'd muck the barn. For a sheltered, refined woman, she wasn't afraid of the hard work that made up most of his days.

He'd never met another woman like her. Cara hadn't been willing to get a little dusty, a little dirty. Cara had never wanted to ride so hard the horses worked themselves into a lather.

Gabriella let out a whoop as Gale charged over a small hill. They were close to the barn, but if he could, he'd watch her ride with this wild abandon all damn day.

And all night. His mind took the view of Gabriella riding hard in the saddle and put it right into his big king bed. Oh, she'd ride him, all right. After that kiss, there wasn't any doubt in his mind about it. He could only hope he could make her whoop and holler as much as racing did.

Far too soon, the barn came into view. He had no idea if Joaquin was behind them—he hadn't hung around to see if the big man had been able to keep up—but he couldn't bring himself to care. His blood was pounding and he couldn't remember feeling this damned happy.

Gabriella slowed Gale to a trot, which meant he had to stop focusing on the way she filled out a saddle and start thinking with his brain again.

"That was so much fun!" she said. "Can we do that to-morrow?"

"You already know what I'm gonna say to that, don't you?"

She gave him the kind of look out of the corner of her eye that made him want to say to hell with Joaquin and guards and what her father might say if he knew she'd kissed him. All he wanted to do was to change course and lead her back to his home—the one that stood silent and empty out on the range, except for when the maid came to clean—and lead her up to his bed.

She was a bright, shining star in the middle of his dark Texas winter and all he wanted to do was to bask in her light. Bask in *her*.

But he also didn't want to die today. So he went a different direction. "Have you managed to get out of the house? I mean, besides to come here."

Some of the light died in her eyes. It hurt him to watch. "I got a haircut, but otherwise, no."

"Tell you what. After we ride tomorrow, I'll take you out. Royal's a nice town. You should see it."

"Really?" Her eyes brightened, but it was short-lived. "Do you think Papa will allow it?"

He was willing to bet the answer was going to be no to that one, but he wasn't about to let something ridiculous like a grown woman asking for parental permission to muck up his date. "Do you want to go out?"

He hadn't asked that particular question in, well, probably close to twenty years. Dates as an adult were more "Can I escort you to an event" than "Going out."

But what was he supposed to do? Part of Gabriella—the social part—still seemed very much the sheltered young girl. No matter how much energy she'd put into kissing him or how good she looked on a horse, he had the feeling he couldn't rush it.

She tilted her head, as if she were debating the question. "Yes," she said, and it did sound like her final answer. "I would like to go out."

Just then, Joaquin came riding up. Beast's sides were heaving and the man on his back looked mad enough to kill Chance the slow, painful way—and, what's more, he looked as though he was going to enjoy doing it.

But before Joaquin could do anything else, Gabriella announced, "Chance will be escorting me out to dinner in Royal tomorrow night, Joaquin," in that same all-business voice.

Joaquin opened his mouth to say something, but she held up a hand and cut him off. "I came here to see America. Chance is merely showing me around."

There was no *merely* about it, not after that kiss. But if that's what it took, then that's what it took. "Yup. You're coming, right?" Because he also had a feeling that trying to cut the big man out was the surest way to not get a date with Gabriella del Toro.

Joaquin towered over them from Beast's big back, clearly displeased with this situation. Would he sign off on Gabriella coming back out to the ranch tomorrow to spend the day hammering iron?

"Or," Gabriella said, and Chance heard a new note in her voice—hard. Stubborn. Suddenly, Gabriella was a woman who could be cruel when she wanted to be—and right now, she wanted to be. "Or I could spend tomorrow cooking. Perhaps I could try lasagna again. I only burned the noodles that one time."

Burned the noodles? Hoo, boy—that sounded like something the hogs wouldn't even eat.

At the look on Joaquin's face, Chance had to bite his tongue to keep from laughing. It was obvious from the way the big guy's lips curled in disgust and he rubbed his chest right where heartburn probably hit him that, despite Gabriella's many talents, cooking was not something she did well.

"The Texas Cattleman's Club has a great restaurant." He said it to Gabriella, but he pitched his voice so that Joaquin would get the message loud and clear. "Some of the best steaks in Texas."

Dang, there was that smile again—the one that made him want to haul her off that horse and kiss her until they both felt like whooping and hollering.

Yeah, he knew what she was playing at. He was only too happy to play along.

The moment that thought crossed his mind, it dragged a different thought along for the ride. What if this—the sob story about her mom, the smiles, especially the kiss—all of it, was just playing? What if she was playing him?

He'd thought Alex Santiago had been one of his best friends—a man he could trust with his life. Where had that gotten him?

Dumped by his lady friend, Cara. The prime suspect in the kidnapping and assault of Alejandro del Toro. A veritable pariah in his hometown.

Alex Santiago—Alejandro del Toro—whoever the hell was locked up in that house—had done his damnedest to screw up Chance's whole life.

How quick had Gabriella del Toro turned on Joaquin to

get what she wanted? He wouldn't have thought a woman could make cooking dinner sound so mean-spirited, but she did.

What if she didn't like him? What if she was trying to muck up the works with her bright smiles and warm looks and sweet, hot kisses? What if she was trying to get him distracted or off balance?

What if she was using him?

But why? That was the question he couldn't answer. Of course, he didn't exactly have a handle as to why Alex had screwed him over, either. All he knew was that he had been screwed over. Royally.

Then Joaquin sighed so heavily that it almost blew Chance's hat off his head.

"Excellent." She did sound awfully damn pleased. But then she added, "I am sure Papa will be so busy with his work he will not notice I am out," in the hurt kind of voice that did its best to rip his heart out of his chest.

He wanted to protect her, by God.

But who would protect him from her?

Gabriella prepared for her date with the greatest of care. She took extra time with her hair and makeup and chose her outfit with Chance in mind.

The day had been something special. She'd met Chance at his barn at nine that morning. They'd taken a slow ride out to Slim's workshop, where Chance had left her and Joaquin for several hours. Then he'd arrived at a quarter to twelve with a basket.

They'd had lunch at the picnic spot. The sun had been just warm enough. Plus, Joaquin had taken his meal leaning back against a tree, which had provided them with enough privacy to have a real conversation as they ate Franny's cold fried chicken and potato salad and drank sweet iced tea.

It had been one of the more romantic events in her life. Just a quiet meal in a secluded, wooded location. She'd almost been able to pretend that Joaquin hadn't been there.

But not so much that she'd done the rash thing and kissed Chance again.

Even though she had wanted to.

After they'd packed up the saddlebags, they'd ridden back to the workshop. Gabriella had made some good progress in hammering. She'd only been able to produce a slightly flat, lumpy piece of wrought iron, but she'd managed to do so with Slim's approval.

Chance had returned for her at three. He'd admired her lump of iron and then offered to race her back to the barn. However, her arms had felt like lead after the work she'd done, so they'd rode at an easy pace.

"I'll pick you up tonight…say, around six-thirty?" is what he'd said from the safety of the saddle.

"Yes. Dinner at your club, correct?"

And he'd flashed her that grin that always made her feel as though she'd returned home after a long, arduous journey. "You betcha."

So now, after one of the best days in her memory, she was trying to gauge what people wore to dine at private clubs in Texas. Was her black pencil skirt and green silk top too much? But they were in Texas. Perhaps it would not be enough. This was the nicest outfit that wasn't a gown and wasn't pants she'd packed. If she threw the matching jacket on over it, she could attend a business meeting with Papa or go to court, if that was what was required.

She was a mess of confusion. She couldn't believe she'd kissed Chance yesterday—and so boldly, in front of Joaquin. That was out of character for her. What was worse, she couldn't believe she *hadn't* kissed him today.

What was she thinking? Chance hadn't been cleared in Alejandro's abduction. Her brother could have been concealed in any one of those buildings—and those were the ones that Chance had chosen to show her. He probably had any number of other buildings across his property.

He'd taken her riding. He'd introduced her to those people who seemed closest to him. Heavens, she was learning to work in wrought iron because he had realized how much she missed her work.

Never before had she felt a man pay such attention to her—her, not her security detail, not to everyone around her.

Just her. When she was with Chance, she felt as if she was the only woman in the world.

As she tried to decide if she would stick with her emerald Tres Cruces set or if she wanted to go with the bold gold necklace that was comprised of a rectangular plate inlaid with emeralds and rubies, someone knocked on her door. "Yes?"

It was Alejandro. He looked better today than he had yesterday and three times better than he had the day before. He seemed to be remembering how to exist in his own skin again after a long holiday somewhere else.

"Alejandro! How are you? Is everything all right?"

He flinched. "Fine," he said, coming in to sit on the end of her bed.

"Are you sure? Do you feel well?"

"No. I just…"

"What? Do you remember something? Something about Chance?"

"No—why?" He looked her over—her tight skirt and the close-cut emerald-green silk top. For her, the outfit displayed a surprising amount of cleavage.

They stared at each other. Gabriella was trying to gauge what her brother might do if he correctly guessed that her interest in Chance McDaniel had nothing to do with the kidnapping. Would he forbid her from seeing Chance? Or

SARAH M. ANDERSON 107

tell Papa—who would then forbid her from seeing Chance again and also subject her to another lecture about her safety being the most important thing?

She could *not* bear another lecture about how her safety was his only priority. What of her happiness? Did that mean nothing to him?

Did that mean anything to Alejandro?

"I want you to call me Alex from now on," Alejandro announced into the tense silence.

"What?"

"Alex. That's my name."

She opened her mouth to ask if he was feeling well or perhaps if he had bumped his head again. But she quickly shut it. The look on her brother's face was not confused or unsure. He was quite serious.

What was she to make of this? He'd said it in that American accent of his. Now that she thought about it, she wasn't sure she'd heard him say a thing in Spanish since she'd arrived in Texas. And now he was choosing his American name.

"I'm going out with Chance tonight." She couldn't imagine another situation where she would be so honest about her feelings, except for this one. "He has also extended an open invitation to ride whenever I so choose and also to join Slim in the workshop, should I wish to learn how to work wrought iron."

Alejandro—Alex—nodded. "Which horse does he have you riding?"

"Nightingale."

Alex gave her a surprised look. "She's one of his prize mares. He doesn't normally let anyone ride her."

"Who did you ride?" It seemed as if a great deal of his memory had "suddenly" returned.

"Quarter horse named Spike. He gave me that horse because he knew his Ranger could always beat Spike."

She grinned at him. "Joaquin rides this massive animal called Beast. I think he may be afraid of the…mule? Yes, mule."

"Beast?" Alex laughed and slapped his knee. It seemed very much the sort of thing Chance would do, but it was not something she could remember her brother doing. How much better was he feeling? "I'd like to see Joaquin afraid of anything!"

"Joaquin does not trust Chance. He does not want me to see him."

Now was the time for honesty. If Alejandro—Alex—oh, heavens, that was going to take some getting used to—objected to her being in Chance's company, he would have to speak his piece or hold it forever.

He did no such thing. Instead he said, "Now that I'm better, Papa expects me to spend more time working with him. He has some deals that are taking up his time."

Although she did not think he meant the words to hurt her, they did anyway. All Papa cared about was that she was safe. After that basic requirement had been met, he cared very little at all.

Alex stood. "I can keep him distracted. There's no need for you to stare at the walls." Gabriella was struck dumb as he walked over to her and placed a brotherly kiss on her forehead. "Go. Have fun."

"I shall," she managed to reply.

Alex turned to leave, but paused with his hand on the doorknob. "I have one request."

"Name it." For the gift he was giving her, she would do anything he asked.

"Take Joaquin, to be safe—and don't tell Chance I'm better. Not yet."

Before she could ask him what he meant by that, he was gone.

The doorbell rang. Chance was here for her.

She knew that Alex would not answer it.

Ten

Chance was feeling good about tonight. Mostly because Gabriella had given him a little peck on the cheek when she'd come to the door, but also because she'd been up in the front seat of his extended cab F-250 and Joaquin had sat in the back.

Chance held the door for Gabriella at the entrance to the Texas Cattleman's Club. He hadn't been here in a long while. Things had gotten to the point where he hadn't been comfortable coming into his favorite hangout. The TCC had become less a place to have a beer than an exercise in navigating shark-infested waters. Better to stay home and eat Franny's cooking or shoot the breeze with Marty and Slim. There, at least, no one treated him like a convicted criminal who hadn't managed to get arrested yet.

Coming here tonight was a risk. But Alex was back. Maybe not all back in the head, but he was no longer missing. People had to have realized that Chance hadn't had a damn thing to do with the whole mess. Right?

He sure as hell hoped so as Joaquin brought up the rear of their little party. Three was starting to be very crowded. But he put on a happy face and guided Gabriella into the TCC.

"They just added the day care," he said, showing Gabriella the new center.

She gave him an odd look as she said, "Very nice," and he realized what he'd said.

They. Not *we.*

"I voted for it," he hurried to add. When had the TCC become a *they*? Probably about the time he'd become a suspect.

Maybe this wasn't such a good idea.

Before he could do anything—point toward the dining room, announce that he'd remembered the restaurant was closed tonight and they should try Claire's instead, a voice called out, "Chance! Where have you been, man?"

Chance whipped around to see Sam Gordon bearing down on them, a huge grin on his face. Someone here was glad to see him. Thank God for small favors. "Sam, you old dog—what's this I hear about Lila?"

"Twins! Girls! Twin girls! Brook was six pounds, six ounces and Eve—she was seven minutes after Brook—was six pounds, four ounces." Sam giggled—a sound that Chance was positive he'd never heard the man make.

"That Lila of yours is quite a woman!" He meant it. Even though there wasn't a lot of love lost between Chance and Beau Hacket, Lila had always gone to great lengths to distance herself from her father and brother. Chance had admired her for striking out on her own and making her own way. A way that now included Sam Gordon.

"I'm so amazed by her." Sam's voice drifted off into sheer awe. But then he snapped back to himself. "Here—cigars for everyone!" And he thrust two cigars at Chance.

Then, a moment later, he offered one to Joaquin. "Here you go, *amigo.*" This time he didn't sound quite so overjoyed.

Sam's gaze darted from Chance to Gabriella to Joaquin—who, after a moment's hesitation, took the proffered cigar with a mumbled, *"Gracias. Felicitaciónes."*

Was this about to go south on him? Only one way to find out. Chance bit the bullet. "Sam Gordon, this is Gabriella del Toro and Joaquin. They're my guests for dinner tonight."

Sam's eyebrows shot so far up at this announcement that they darn near cleared his forehead. "Well, a pleasure to meet you, Ms. del Toro." But he didn't offer his hand. Instead he sort of bowed—without taking his eyes off Joaquin *or* the slight bulge in his jacket where his gun was. "Uh, how is Alex? Or is it Alejandro?"

Chance felt Gabriella stiffen beside him, but her face betrayed no other emotion than pleasantness. It was the exact same expression she'd had on her face when he'd walked into Alex's house and found her the first time.

Then, he hadn't noticed anything was wrong. Now? Now that he'd spent his afternoons riding with her and had meals with her and seen the real her? Now he could tell that she was nervous. Unsure of what to do next.

He could sympathize.

"Thank you for your concern," she finally said in her soft voice. "He is doing better. And he prefers to be called Alex."

"Okay, great—good to hear." Sam and Gabriella made a little more small talk about babies, but Chance wasn't paying attention.

Instead he was staring at Gabriella. They'd spent a better part of the past week together and she'd said nothing about Alex wanting to be called Alex. She'd called him Alejandro when they were together. Always.

Whenever he asked about Alex, she said he was the same. When had he decided he wanted to be called Alex? And why hadn't she told Chance that?

Was she lying to Sam? Or had she been lying to him?

Damn.

"Well, see you around, old dog," Sam said as he clapped Chance on the back.

"And congratulations again on the girls," Chance said as Sam left them.

The three of them stood there for a second. Across the room, Chance noticed Paul Windsor talking to some of his buddies. He'd spent time with Paul when he and Cara had been dating. Paul was a nice enough fellow, but Chance hadn't liked the man's attitude toward his daughter—as if she were merely a pawn to be used as he saw fit for the family business, Windsor Energy. Chance had always had the feeling that he didn't bring enough to the table for Cara and that, if the relationship had gotten that far, Paul wouldn't have given him permission to ask for Cara's hand in marriage.

Since Chance had become a suspect in Alex Santiago's disappearance, Paul Windsor had acted plenty justified in feeling that Chance had never been good enough for Cara. Paul had been one of the first to question Chance's possible motives. Hell, it was almost as if the man wanted Chance to take the blame.

Paul glanced across the space and met Chance's eyes before he turned a mercenary look to Gabriella. Something cold flittered over his face and, with a smile that bordered on cruel, turned back to his conversation. The whole thing had taken ten seconds, tops, but a worried pit in Chance's stomach made him think there'd been something else going on—something beyond Paul Windsor feeling justified that Chance as a kidnapping suspect proved that he'd never been good enough for Cara.

Chance didn't like this. He didn't like always feeling guilty until proved innocent and he sure as hell didn't like feeling the same way about Gabriella. He didn't want to think she was anything like her brother. He wanted to believe that she'd been nothing but up front with him—that everything she'd said was the truth, the whole truth and nothing but the truth.

Except that every time he started to believe that, she'd do something that threw her whole character into question. Such as tell Sam Gordon instead of Chance that her brother was Alex and not Alejandro.

Damn it all.

He skipped the rest of the tour and ushered them toward the restaurant. For a Monday, the place was hopping. Over half the tables were full, and warm laughter filled the room. As the server lead them to a table—for three, double damn it—the laughter died off as people watched him walk with the traitor Alex's sister and her armed thug.

It made a part of him ache. Would he ever get to feel as though he was part of this again? Or would he always be tainted by someone else's guilt?

Yeah, this had been an epic mistake. But it was too late now. Everyone knew he was here and, between Sam Gordon and Paul Windsor, they probably all knew who Gabriella was, to boot. He had no choice but to brazen this out. McDaniels did not tuck tail and run.

He let Joaquin have the seat with his back to the wall and held the chair for Gabriella so that she could have a nice view of the room. He put his back to the room as a sign to Joaquin that he wasn't worried.

They placed their orders and waited. Long gone was the easy conversation from the picnic lunch today. Instead Gabriella sat with her hands primly folded in her lap, her shoulders back and that blankly pleasant look on her face. To a stranger—to most of the people in this room—she would look perfectly normal.

But he could tell she wasn't. Her lips were pressed together extra hard, without a trace of the easy smile that she favored him with.

At least Joaquin pretty much looked and acted the same as always—grumpy, borderline violent and put out to be here.

Every so often, Chance would hear his name. He'd crane around in his seat only to realize that no one was talking *to* him—they were talking *about* him. All of Paul Windsor's cronies appeared to be working overtime to spread God only knew what kind of rumors about him. Or Gabriella. Or, worse yet, him *and* Gabriella. He didn't want to guess what they were saying about Joaquin.

No one came over to talk. Sam Gordon had been a fluke, that much was obvious. Instead people waved at him and went back to whatever gossip they were intent on spreading like manure on a field.

The waitress brought their food. After several minutes of silent eating, Gabriella set her knife and fork aside and folded her hands in her lap again. "What's the matter?" Had this evening gone so wrong that even the food had not lived up to expectations?

She sighed, but her shoulders didn't slump down in defeat. Just a lone little weary sigh. "Is it that they are afraid of me? Or you?"

"I don't think they're afraid of either of us. Maybe Joaquin." At this, the big man managed to actually look guilty. "Sorry. It's just…this is a small town. Word gets around fast."

"Ah." She dropped her gaze, the barest hint of color in her cheeks. "We are the evening's entertainment?"

"It's my fault. I thought…" Well, he'd thought people might be decent, or at least give him the benefit of the doubt.

He decided to change the subject. "He wants to be called Alex now, does he?"

The color in her cheeks deepened. Why did she have to be so beautiful? Why did he have to be so attracted to her? Why couldn't things be simpler, as they'd been long before Alex Santiago had mucked up his world?

"He seems to respond better to that name. I'm…" She swallowed. She was about to lie to him, he realized. He could see it coming and couldn't do a damn thing about it. "I'm hoping it will help his recovery to stick to the name that draws a more positive reaction from him."

"Is that a fact." It wasn't a question.

"Yes." She cleared her throat. By now her cheeks were redder than a tomato in August. But she lifted her head, that blank pleasantness almost a challenge to him. "I do not wish to speak of him tonight."

That meant she wasn't going to try to backtrack out of her lie. But it also meant she wasn't going to tell him another one. "Well, you just let me know when you do wish to speak of him, okay?"

The look of pain that bled the beautiful right out of her blush made him feel like a jerk. But he wasn't the one who was being jerky here, was he? She'd told the lie. She expected him to go along with it? He was an honest fellow. He was not the bad guy here.

Yeah, dinner had been a mistake.

"It's not like that." Her voice was so soft he almost didn't hear her.

"You tell me what it's like, then. You know why we're the evening's entertainment? It's because your brother—him of which we do not speak—rolled into town and decided I was an easy mark. He set me up, stole my girl and disappeared, leaving me to deal with the wreckage."

Joaquin shot him a look and Chance realized that his voice might have gotten a little louder. Okay, a lot louder. But damn it, he was tired of being the one everyone gossiped about. He wanted his name cleared so things could go back to normal.

Back to being lonely.

No. He pushed back against that thought, against the thought of Gabriella astride Gale. Against the quiet of the picnic lunch today. So what if he'd had more fun in the past week than he'd had in months? So what if Franny adored her and Slim thought she was "somethin'"? So what if Gabriella had kissed him as though her life depended on it—and if he'd thought of nothing but ever since?

None of that mattered. She'd go back to Mexico and he'd still be here in Royal, dealing with the wreckage.

Too late, he realized the restaurant was silent. Everyone was listening to them now.

"Let's just go," he said. It came out as a snarl, but what the hell.

"Yes." She stood, as composed as ever. Only the slightest downturn at the corner of her mouth gave her away. "Let's."

The drive home was painful. He pulled up in front of Alex's house. In the dark, the place had a malicious look to it, as if it had already eaten Alex and was waiting to swallow Gabriella, too.

He put the truck in park but didn't shut it off. Which made him feel even worse. He *was* being a jerk now, not even offering to walk her to the door. That's why she had an armed guard, right?

"Joaquin," she said in her all-business voice. "Please go check on Alex."

The big man huffed behind Chance and made no move to exit the vehicle.

"Now, please. I wish to speak to Chance alone." It was the most polite order he'd ever heard anyone give.

Yeah, Chance said silently to himself. He had a few things he wanted to say without risking a near-death experience. *Get out of the truck, man.*

Joaquin didn't.

Gabriella turned to glare at her guard. "I am twenty-seven years of age, Joaquin. I have the right to have a private conversation without having it reported back to my father. Stop treating me like a child or I will have you reassigned." She leaned back, her voice dropping a dangerous octave. "And I *will* have you reassigned."

Man, if he'd thought the silence had been heavy before, it was downright crushing now. But he didn't want to say anything. This was clearly between the two of them and it sure looked as though Gabriella could defend herself.

Then, unexpectedly, Joaquin yielded. The truck door opened and shut, and he was gone. He crossed in front of the truck and shot Chance a mean look before he walked up the path to the front door. But the door didn't open. So they weren't truly alone.

Before Chance could determine how much Joaquin could see from his perch on the porch a good fifty feet away, Gabriella grabbed him and hauled his face down to hers. The kiss this time was different—instead of the happy-to-the-point-of-ecstatic kiss that she'd given him yesterday, this one had an edge to it. As though she was trying to prove something.

He couldn't tell who she was trying to prove it to—him or herself.

Well, she could keep on trying. He wasn't playing this game. He kept his hands on the wheel.

When her tongue traced his lips, his resolve started to waver. It wavered a whole hell of a lot more when she slid her fingers up into his hair. The feeling of her hands on him did some mighty funny things to him. In fact, the things that were happening below his belt were freaking *hilarious*.

He couldn't think. Well, he could, but that wasn't thinking in a right sense. Instead of thinking about whether or not he could trust her, he was thinking about the way her teeth felt as she nipped at his lower lip.

She pulled away. He couldn't believe how much it hurt to let her do it, but he kept his white-knuckled grip on the steering wheel. Hell, he was lucky he hadn't snapped the whole thing off the steering column at this rate.

"Do you want me?" she breathed as she ran her fingers over his cheeks. Her chest was heaving and, in that top, that was saying something. She sounded seductive—hell, she *was* seductive—but there was something else in her eyes. It almost looked as though she was afraid of what he might say.

Was it a trick question? Because the answer was *yes*. She may be setting him up but he wasn't sure he gave a damn.

Don't be an idiot. He hadn't asked enough questions when he'd let Cara go. He needed answers almost as much as he needed to pull her into his arms.

"I want the woman who likes to ride and work metal and laughs like butterflies in the breeze. I don't want the woman who hides lies behind a blank smile."

He felt her pull away, even though her hands stayed on him. "I am the woman who rides and works metal." Then she let go of him—but only long enough to duck under his arm that was still holding on to the steering wheel for dear life. She straddled him. Her slim black skirt—the one that made her backside look even better than a pair of jeans ever could—bunched up at her hips. "That's who I am."

His arms were shaking from the effort of *not* touching her. Because he wasn't. No way in hell. She was doing this. She was doing *all* of this.

She leaned her forehead against him. Her thighs—strong from years of riding—gripped his and he felt the tantalizing heat of her center through his jeans. How strong did one man have to be? Because a lesser man would wrap his arms around her and take what she was offering.

But taking a woman with an audience—if Joaquin was

still watching from the stoop or if he'd gone inside and alerted Alex or her father of what was happening—was too stupid of a risk to take. So, even though it was the most painful thing he could remember doing—way more painful than getting kicked by that calf in the shin when he was ten—he kept his hands on the steering wheel.

It only got worse when she kissed him again—a kiss that started out soft and gentle and maybe even a little hesitant—just like her. Then it got hot, fast. Her hips ground down on his and she pressed those beautiful breasts against his chest. Only some lousy clothes separated them. That was not a whole lot and way, *way* too much.

He pulled his head back, but the rest of him had no place to go. She had him pinned. "Don't lie to me, Gabriella. I won't stand for it."

She nodded, looking sad and sensual at the same time. That, almost more than her sweet body or sweeter face, made him want to wrap her up and hold her tight. "This is the truth, Chance. I ride. I work metal. And you make me laugh. That's who I am. That's who I get to be with you." Her fingers traced a path from his cheeks to his jaw, as though she was exploring him when what she was really doing was burning him with her touch. "No one else. Just you."

He shouldn't believe her. She was setting him up and sooner or later, he was going to fall—hard.

Hell, he was already falling for the woman who'd had smudges of soot on her forehead the whole time they'd sat by the bank of his dry creek. He was already falling for the woman who was perfectly comfortable chatting with Franny or working with Slim, for the woman who saddled her own horse and rode hell-for-leather.

He wanted that woman to be the one in his arms. God, he'd never wanted anything so bad.

Then she said in a breathy whisper, "That's who I am, because of you," and he felt lost to her.

This time, he was the one doing the kissing. He managed to keep his hands on the wheel because if he didn't, he'd be pulling her shirt over her head and trying to get his buckle undone and filling his hands with her soft skin.

Yeah, it was probably going to get him beat to a pulp, but he didn't give a damn. It was worth it to feel her passion surging against him, to feel the heat of her body setting his on fire. He wanted to bury himself in her and make her cry out with pleasure. He wanted to surrender himself to her in a way that he had never wanted to before. Anything was worth this moment with her.

Anything she asked of him was hers.

So when she said, "Can I come back to the ranch tomorrow?" all he could do was kiss her again, feel the way her body fit over his.

"You already knew the answer. All you had to do was ask."

Her face lit up into a wide smile, the kind that couldn't be faked. "Thank you." She said it in words and with another kiss.

He needed to say good-night to her and walk her to the door. But he couldn't help taking another kiss from her. And another. And just one more. He couldn't quite get enough of her. Everything about her overrode his better judgment. Even if things were as normal as possible—Gabriella was still Alex's little sister. And a man had to tread lightly when it came to making out in a truck with his best friend's sister.

Then, unexpectedly, a light came on in the house. It wasn't a spotlight that hit them in the truck or anything, but it meant someone was moving around in the front of the house. Someone who might see them.

Both Chance and Gabriella reacted at the same time,

jolting against each other. Which made him groan in frustration. Another day with Gabriella, another night in unsatisfied agony.

"I should go," she said in a near whisper.

"Yeah." *No.*

She slid off his lap and lifted her bottom off the seat so she could pull her skirt back down.

How far gone was he? So far that he almost slid his hand up her exposed leg, almost cupped that curvy bottom in his hands and *almost* pulled her right back onto his lap.

"I'll walk you up." It was the least he could do. Plus, it'd give him another few minutes of being close to her.

They got out of the car. She adjusted her skirt one final time, then held out her hand to him. They walked up to the front step, where Joaquin stood, waiting. He glared at Chance extra hard, but Chance ignored the big man. "You want to do some more work in the shop tomorrow?"

One of her fingers traced over his knuckle. It sent a jolt of heat through him that not even Joaquin could temper. "But of course."

"What time can I expect you?" The more important question was, what time would she leave? She'd come home today to change for the date disaster. He had no desire to repeat dinner at the club. But that didn't mean he was out of options.

When she didn't answer immediately, he jumped into the gap. "Franny would be happy to make us dinner, or we could try Claire's." Even in the dim light, he could see the look of terror cross her face. "Claire's is different. Quieter." More dimly lit, more private. People went to the TCC to see and be seen. People went to Claire's when they didn't want to look at anyone but the other person at their table. And he didn't want to look at anyone but Gabriella.

He hadn't been to Claire's since...well, since he'd given Cara his blessing to start seeing Alex. They'd had their first date at the restaurant, and it had seemed fitting to bring the relationship full circle. Since then, he hadn't had anyone he wanted to take.

Plus, at Claire's it wouldn't be a big deal if Joaquin sat at a different table. No more of this three's-a-crowd crap.

"If you say Claire's will be fine, I trust you." He could see that the prospect of another outing into greater Royal still made her nervous, but at least she wasn't hiding behind that blankness again.

"I've got meetings all morning with people about a wedding—including a tasting for lunch. If you came out after lunch, we could go straight to dinner."

She frowned, her lips twisted into a displeased grimace. "In case you didn't notice, by the time I get done at the furnace, I'm in no shape to be seen."

"I don't know about that." Before he could stop himself, he reached up and touched her forehead, where she'd had the smudge earlier this afternoon. Her lips twisted even more, but he could see that she was trying hard not to smile at him—and failing. "But don't forget, I live right there. You could use my shower to get cleaned up." He swallowed, knowing full well Joaquin was memorizing every word.

The look on her face made it real clear that she didn't want to come all the way back here. He understood—he'd gone out with a girl in high school who'd had a rough dad. Their dates had always started the minute the final school bell rang. Coming home had meant another chance to be stopped by her father. Obviously it was the same for Gabriella.

Chance didn't know if Rodrigo del Toro was a violent man. But he sure as hell wasn't pleasant to be around.

"I would like that." She leaned up and brushed her lips across his. It took more than effort than he liked to keep from sweeping her into his arms and kissing the hell out of her. But he managed to keep the brakes on. "Tomorrow, then."

"Tomorrow," he called to her as she strode past Joaquin and into the house.

The big man favored Chance with another murderous glare before he turned and slammed the door in Chance's face.

Yeah.

Man, he couldn't remember the last time he'd looked this forward to a Tuesday.

Eleven

The moment the door shut, Gabriella spun on her guard. "You are out of line, Joaquin. *Out of line.*"

Joaquin glared at her, but he did not respond.

Gabriella could not remember being madder than she was at this precise moment. There were many times she had been upset. When her brother had been granted permission to get his own apartment in Mexico City, she'd been beyond furious. And not because he was moving out for good.

Because the announcement had been book-ended by her father's decision that she not be allowed to go to university. For her safety, of course.

Gabriella had rebelled long and hard. She'd cut her hair off with a pair of shears, leaving her beautiful tresses on the ground and what was left on her head an uneven mess. She'd gotten tattoos all over her arms and neck. True, they'd been drawn on with pen instead of with a needle, but it had been worth it for the look of horror on her father's face.

It had taken weeks for the drawings to wash away, years for her hair to grow back.

She'd wanted to go to university for the sake of going— for being anywhere but home. It hadn't been that different than any other teenage girl wanting to spread her wings and fly.

Normally, when she was upset, she threatened Joaquin with small things—her cooking, shoe shopping. It was a little game they played with each other. She had long since stopped asking for things she knew she would not get and fought only the small things she could.

This was different. This was not for the sake of going. No man—with the possible exception of Joaquin himself—had ever paid this kind of attention to her. Treated her as anything more than a fine china doll to be locked in a case and gazed at on occasion.

Chance treated her like the flesh-and-blood woman she was.

She had not lied to Chance. When she was on his ranch, riding his horse, working in his shop, she felt like the woman she always wanted to be. It wasn't that different than what she did at home. But a picnic lunch? Dinners out?

A man who made her blood sing? Who saw her first and her family name last?

She would fight for that.

"I want to be with him. Are you going to stop me?"

Joaquin flinched, his jaw set. But still he did not speak.

She heard noises overhead. She had only a matter of moments before her father or brother came down. If it was Papa, he might start questioning where she'd been, who she'd been with. She did not want to lie to him. He may have kept her wrapped up like a china doll he was afraid of dropping but she still loved him.

"Are you going to tell on me as if I'm a little girl?"

Joaquin dropped his gaze to his shoes and she knew he would. The white-hot rage that coursed through her was only tempered by a wave of sadness. She might get to see

Chance for a while, but sooner or later it would come to an end.

Sooner or later, she'd be put back in her glass case, a fragile thing to be protected above all else.

"After all this time—all the years you've stood by my side—I thought you might want me to be happy. I thought… I thought you might work for me. Not for Papa."

He did not correct her. In fact, he did nothing but continue to stare at the tips of his shoes.

Ah.

Her time with Chance was limited. Her path and his would not cross again once she returned to Mexico. But she would have even less time now than she'd hoped.

She might only get one more day. One more evening to feel as special, as *free,* as he made her feel.

She had best make the most of it.

Chance sat in his living room across from Joaquin. Upstairs, he could hear the running water in his shower.

The shower that currently contained one very nude Gabriella del Toro.

If this were any other situation, Chance wouldn't be in the middle of a staring match with a man. He'd have shucked his own clothes and offered his services in washing her back. And her front. And all the parts in between.

To hell with dinner. They'd never make it past the top step.

And yet, here he sat. With Joaquin.

If it were any other woman, this wouldn't be worth it.

But Gabriella was.

At least the place was clean. His home wasn't the Ritz, but the old place suited him just fine. Three bedrooms upstairs, with a kitchen, dining room and parlor downstairs. And he'd had Lupe come in today and give it a thorough once-over. He hoped Gabriella thought it was okay.

He heard the water shut off. God, she was probably rubbing a towel all over her wet body. Then sliding into a pair of little lacy panties. Settling her full breasts into an equally lacy bra. Would she be zipping up another body-hugging skirt or maybe a pair of tight slacks?

Although he didn't move, Chance was pretty sure Joaquin made a noise of displeasure in the back of his throat. Great.

"You know I'm not going to hurt her, right?"

Joaquin raised an eyebrow in what looked a hell of a lot like disbelief.

"And that I didn't do a thing to her brother?"

The other eyebrow went up. Yeah, Joaquin didn't believe a word he said.

Chance sighed. He'd have a more successful conversation with his horse. "I just want her to be happy. That's all. That doesn't make me the bad guy here."

At this, Joaquin's face—well, it didn't crumble. Chance wasn't sure he even moved a muscle. But he went from looking dangerous to looking…sheepish? Was that possible?

"Ready," Gabriella called from the top of the stairs.

Chance and Joaquin stood at the same time as Gabriella made her way downstairs. She had on a cream-colored skirt with a purple top and a pair of purple shoes. The skirt cupped her bottom and flared out, while the top didn't have sleeves. Everything clung to her like a second skin.

Yeah, if it wasn't for the bodyguard, they wouldn't make it out of the house tonight.

"What do you think?" Gabriella spun in a slow circle for Chance. That's when he saw that her top also didn't have a whole lot of fabric in the back. It was one of those halter tops that tied at the neck and left most of her back bare and begging to be touched.

Man, did he want to touch.

"Well?" She'd turned back to face him again, her smile both knowing and somehow coy.

He managed to drag his eyes away from where he could now clearly see her nipples outlined in the thin fabric. "I don't want you to get cold." There. That was a reasonable thing to say that didn't sound as if he was a slobbering horn-dog teenager who couldn't get past the fact that she wasn't wearing a bra.

"Oh! The jacket! I'll be right back."

Chance was treated to the view of Gabriella's legs and backside climbing the stairs. Wow. *Wow.* He wanted to get to dinner. The sooner they ate, the sooner they could come back.

At least, he hoped they were coming back. When Gabriella reappeared in a matching cream-colored jacket, he was relieved to see that she didn't have the bag of toiletries she'd packed. Good. She was coming back here tonight to get her things. The question was, how long would she stay?

More importantly, what would he do when she left?

Yeah, that was the question of the day. Of the month.

"Shall we?" He managed to get the door opened.

"Is it all right if Joaquin drives?" Gabriella's voice was light as she said this, but Chance heard an undercurrent of tension.

Was she nervous about dinner? He'd called ahead and reserved two tables, including the most private table in the restaurant, one tucked back in a little nook. He was lucky that Valentine's Day had passed. There was no way he would have gotten that table on such short notice before that.

If Joaquin drove, they'd have to bring him home, right? He could only hope the big man wouldn't make him walk the fifteen miles. "That's fine." He held the back door of the big SUV open for her as Joaquin clomped around to the driver's side door. Then, once Gabriella had slid in, he climbed in after her.

And was thrilled to find that she hadn't scooted all the way over to the other side. Instead she sat right in the middle—close enough to touch.

So he shut the door, buckled up and touched. He draped his arm around her shoulder and pulled her tighter against him.

She sighed, her body molding itself to him. She rested her head on his shoulder and then placed her left hand on his thigh. It wasn't an overt come-on, but the feeling of her curled into him was more than enough to drive him to distraction.

Even though he was not, in fact, driving, he still had to make sure they got to where they were going. So, with Gabriella holding on to him as tightly as he was holding on to her, he gave Joaquin directions to Claire's.

The whole time, he kept wondering how much longer he'd have. How much longer until Alex started feeling better? Until they caught the bastards that had kidnapped him in the first place? Until the entire del Toro family packed up and went south of the border?

How much longer would he have to look forward to saddling up with Gabriella and riding the range? To finding her all smudged and happy from another day spent at the furnace in Slim's shop? To seeing her get all dressed up for a night out on the town?

He laced his fingers with hers. Her hands weren't the babied softness of a woman who was afraid of work, afraid of messing up her manicure. They were clean but she had calluses on the sides of her fingers and a few small scars on the back where she'd probably caught a piece of hot metal at some point.

God, he hoped he wasn't making the biggest mistake of his life.

They arrived at Claire's right at six-thirty. Chance didn't wait to see if Joaquin would open the door for them. He didn't think it'd go over real well if he started treating the big man like a chauffeur. So he hopped out and held out a hand for Gabriella.

He didn't let go of her once she'd gotten her feet under her, either. He was tired of pretending he wasn't interested in her. The little "conversation" in the front seat of his truck last night made pretending pointless.

"Hello, Mr. McDaniel." The hostess gave them a polite smile and added, "This way, please," before anyone could say anything else.

Gabriella's hand tightened around his as they walked into the restaurant. "You called ahead?"

"I'm not leaving anything to chance tonight." That included condoms. Hell, he didn't know if they'd get to that point—or how—but after the way she'd straddled him last night?

She shot him a red-hot smile. "Good thinking."

Oh, yeah.

The place wasn't packed but it wasn't empty, either. Chance saw Ryan Grant sitting with a beautiful redhead. It wasn't until he waved and Ryan waved back that the woman turned—and he recognized Piper Kindred.

"Friends?" Gabriella asked, her grip tightening on his.

"Yup." Obviously, Ryan and Piper were here on a date. Just like Chance and Gabriella.

So Chance tipped his hat to Ryan and Piper and led Gabriella away and back to the secluded table.

"Enjoy," their hostess said.

She motioned Joaquin to a small table on the other side of the aisle. The big man could keep an eye on them—and the rest of the restaurant—but he wasn't at their table. That's all Chance wanted.

Well, it wasn't all he wanted.

But it was what he would take for at the moment.

Gabriella settled into the chair that Chance held for her and focused on breathing. She couldn't even see the couple that Chance had recognized earlier. She had no way of knowing if they were talking about him—or her. But the greetings had seemed friendly and neither the man nor the woman had given her the kind of look that she'd gotten last night at the club—the vicious, gleeful kind of look that went with gossip.

"Wine?" Chance asked, looking over the list.

"Yes, please." He seemed more relaxed here than he had at the club last night. She needed to be the same.

She wanted to be the same. Alex had managed to keep Papa busy this morning. She had come up with every single menial errand and task that Joaquin could do for her to keep him too busy to have a private word with Papa. But she knew she couldn't do that all day, every day. Sooner or later, Joaquin would provide a status update to Papa and her time with Chance would end.

So she had to make the most of tonight. She *would* make the most of it.

But first, wine.

They ordered—he got the prime rib, she ordered the black and blue steak salad with a bottle of Shiraz to share. She was trying not to look at Joaquin. She wanted this illusion of freedom, didn't she? She wanted this taste of a life outside of her father's control.

She wanted Chance.

Judging from the way his jaw had dropped when she'd first walked down the stairs in her slinkiest top, he wanted her, too.

That was what she needed to focus on. Not the roiling nerves that had her stomach in a state of distress and not whatever anyone else in the restaurant may or may not be saying about her and Chance.

Just the way he'd looked at her, as if she was the only woman in the world. As if he'd wanted to sweep her into his arms and carry her right back up to that big bed in his room—because of course she'd peeked in and looked at how big his bed was. More than big enough for two people. The coverlet was a quilt done in blues and whites—old-fashioned, yes, but well loved and well taken care of. It had seemed perfectly in place in his home.

She wanted to get back to that bed tonight.

She glanced up at Chance and found him staring at her. "Yes?"

"You look amazing tonight."

She felt the heat of the blush rush to her cheeks, but she didn't try to distract from it with a soft platitude. Instead she let the smile take hold of her lips. "Thank you."

He leaned forward. "Do you know how much longer you're going to be in Royal?"

"Until Alex has been cleared by his doctors and the police to return." Of course, Alex would have to actually meet with the doctors and officers to be cleared for travel—something he seemed in no great hurry to do.

"So you don't know when you're going to leave." It didn't quite sound like a question—more like a rumination.

"No."

"And you'll go back to your estate near Mexico City?"

"Yes." Why was he asking about her travel plans?

"Do you ever leave the estate? Do you travel?"

She regarded him for a moment. "I go into the city for gallery openings. That occurs once or twice a year."

"How about visitors? Do you ever have visitors at the estate?"

Gabriella couldn't help herself. She glanced at Joaquin,

who was staring at both of them, as was expected. "Why do you ask?"

Chance looked down at his hands. He'd started rubbing his knuckles, as if he were looking for a fight.

Or as if he were nervous.

"It's just that..." He cleared his throat and reached his hand halfway across the table, waiting for her to place her hand in his. "Please, Gabriella."

He *was* nervous. That had the direct effect of making her nervous.

But she couldn't resist the pull of his hand. She let the tips of her fingers skim over his palm before they locked hands together.

"I haven't had a serious relationship in a while. I mean, yeah, I was dating Cara Windsor, but that was more because we were friends who got on well. I couldn't see her making a place for herself out on the ranch. She didn't like riding and was more than a little afraid of Slim."

"Why are you telling me this?" She did not wish to speak of old girlfriends. She may not have a great deal of dating experience, but she was reasonably sure that this was the wrong way to seduce someone.

"Because after Cara left me for Alex, I told myself I was done. There weren't too many women left in Royal who'd cotton to my way of living. I get up before dawn in the summer and don't sit back down until the sun sets. I smell like horse and cow and dirt for most of the day."

He was pouring his heart out, of that much she was certain. But... "What does 'cotton' mean?" She felt dumb for asking, but she recalled Slim saying that about his given name and she hadn't yet figured out what it meant.

The grin that he gave her put her at ease. He didn't think she was dumb for asking. "Take to. Like. No one else in this town cares to live the kind of life I live. Cara is a wonderful woman, but that's not the kind of life she wanted and we both knew it. She was happier with your brother. That was the life she wanted and I accepted that."

She flinched. She couldn't help it. Talking about Alex would mean that she would either have to lie to Chance or betray her brother's confidences, and she did not want to do either of those things. "I do not wish to speak of him. Not now."

He nodded in agreement. "I don't, either. I want you to understand. After Cara and I were done, I'd…I'd given up hoping that there was a woman in this world who would fit in mine."

He tightened his grip on her as he lifted his gaze to meet her. His eyes—those beautiful bright green eyes that always made her feel as though she'd come home—made her want to do far more than hold hands.

His mouth crooked in a smile. "Then I met you. And everything changed."

The air rushed out of her lungs as she gripped his hand with all her might. She felt as if she might fall out of her chair otherwise.

This…this was being seduced. His words took all of her worries and pushed them right out of her head. Who cared about old girlfriends or injured brothers? She didn't.

She cared for Chance.

"I know we can't keep doing this forever," he went on, dropping his gaze back to where their hands were connected. He turned her hand over and started rubbing his thumb over her wrist, sending delicious shivers up her back. "I know it'll come to an end and you'll be in Mexico and I'll be in Texas. But that doesn't mean we have to let this die on the vine."

She wasn't sure what "die on the vine" meant, but she was very sure she didn't care. "What are you saying?"

"My life is here. That land has been in my family for over a hundred years and I can't walk away from that. But

I don't want to let you go, Gabriella. If you want me to, I'll come see you. We have slow times where I can get away for a week or two. And you're always welcome at the ranch."

She opened her mouth to say something—but the problem was she didn't know what to say. Not with him speaking words such as these.

Words no man had ever said to her. No man had ever *tried* to say to her. No man had ever gone out of his way to accommodate her structured lifestyle. That Chance would make the effort was, in and of itself, an impressive act.

Then he swallowed. "What I'm saying is, I'm falling in love with you and I don't want to let that go when you leave Texas."

"¡Dios mío!" she heard herself breathe. Did he just say he was in love? With *her?*

His crooked grin got a little more worried. "Did you mean that in a good way?"

When she still couldn't come up with a reasonable response, he leaned away from her. But he didn't let her go. "If you don't feel the same, I understand. You've got a lot to deal with as it is and it's not my place to make your life more complicated than it already is. No harm, no foul."

He started to pull his hand away from hers, but she refused to let him. So she was having trouble finding the words. There were other ways to express herself.

That was how she came to be half out of her chair, reaching across the table until she had grabbed Chance's shirt in her hands and hauled him to her. She crushed her lips to his.

Yes, this—this was exactly what she wanted. The words of love—not words she read in a book or watched two characters say to each other in a telenovela, but words spoken directly to her. About her.

At this precise moment, nothing else mattered. Not Joaquin sitting ten feet away, not the other people dining in the restaurant. She did not care what her brother or her father might say about such a bold action on her behalf.

All she cared about—all she wanted to care about—was Chance falling in love with her.

She was falling in love with Chance.

But the kiss was awkward over the table and only became more so when the waitress arrived with their meals.

Gabriella let go of Chance and sat with a thud in her chair. The two of them stared at each other for a moment as the waitress tried to act as if she hadn't seen anything unusual at all.

Then Chance turned his attention to the server. "Can we get the food wrapped up to go? Quickly?"

The waitress smirked but said, "Of course," as she picked up the tray and disappeared into the kitchen.

"You wanna get out of here?"

Gabriella didn't bother to look at Joaquin. She already knew he would not be happy with this turn of events. For all she knew, she was only hastening the day when Papa would not let her see Chance again with her brazen behavior.

But she would have this night with him, one way or the other.

"Yes," she said.

And that was final.

Twelve

Somehow they got out of the restaurant and into her SUV. It seemed as though Joaquin was in no hurry to drive them anywhere, but Chance didn't give a flying damn. They left the big man in the restaurant and hustled to the car. Chance was in the backseat with Gabriella and the windows were tinted. Close enough.

He managed to get the door shut behind them and to set the boxed-up meals down behind the seat before his hands were all over Gabriella.

And, boy, her hands were all over him as she fell back against the seat and pulled him on top of her. She grabbed his backside and pulled him into her, pushing her skirt up. Despite the clothing, he could feel the warm heat of her core. Her hands worked their way up from his butt to his back as she felt his muscles.

Her touch alone was enough to push him right up to the edge of his control. Combine that with the way her legs slid around him? Damn. "I want you so much," he whispered as he propped himself up on his arms. This had the nice effect of pushing his erection harder against her warmth. "*So* much."

"Yes. Me, too. Oh, yes," she moaned as he pivoted his hips, tested the limits of his pants. "Oh, Chance."

Hearing her mouth say his name that way—as though he meant everything to her—was all he wanted. Yeah, the sex would be amazing, he didn't doubt that. But he wanted so much more than that.

Her. That was all.

His tongue swept into her mouth as he managed to balance himself so that he could touch her generous breasts. Nope, no bra—and he'd never been happier. He stroked her through the thin fabric and was rewarded when her nipple went rock-hard.

"Yeah," he said as her hips bucked against his. "Just like that. God, you're beautiful, Gabriella. Tell me what you like. Everything you want."

Her hands stilled against him. Something seemed off as she said, "Chance..." but before she could finish her thought, the driver's side door opened.

Crap on toast. Joaquin. Chance had been so wrapped up in Gabriella—literally and figuratively—that he'd actually forgotten about the big man. And the fact that they were still in a car.

He sat up so Gabriella could get herself put back together. Joaquin seemed to be doing the same thing—he hadn't gotten into the vehicle yet.

Shuddering, Gabriella managed to get her skirt rearranged. Then she said, "Joaquin, please take us back to Chance's house," in a voice that didn't sound embarrassed. A little happy, but not embarrassed.

Maybe sneaking around the hired help was something she was used to. If she wasn't going to act guilty about this, then he wasn't, either.

He wasn't sure Joaquin was on board, though. Now that Chance had himself under control—okay, *more* under control—he could see the big man glaring at him from where he stood outside the door.

"Please," Gabriella repeated. This time Chance heard a note of desperation in her voice.

"I'm not going to hurt her," Chance added, unsure if he should be saying anything.

But he didn't want to sit here in the back of this vehicle in what was, essentially, a Mexican standoff with an actual Mexican. He wanted to get someplace that had a locking door and pillows, and he wanted to get there sooner rather than later.

That wasn't Joaquin's idea of a good evening, apparently. The next thing Chance knew, Gabriella had jolted forward and was half draped over the front passenger seat. "This is my choice. I choose to go home with him and I choose to go to bed with him. There is nothing you can do tonight that will stop me. You can either guard me as you have sworn to do or leave me alone and go back to Papa."

Boy, he loved it when she was fiery—except for that one word: *tonight*. He didn't like that word. It begged the question—what could Joaquin do tomorrow to keep Gabriella from him?

"Fine." She turned to Chance, her eyes flashing with righteous fury. "Get out."

"What?"

"Your friends in the restaurant—would they give us a ride home?"

Chance's mouth flopped open. "Uh…"

"Or taxis? Do you have taxis in this town?"

"Sure." Boy, remind him not to get on Gabriella's bad side. He wasn't surprised that Rodrigo lived up to the family name—del Toro was "of the bull"—but for the first time, he truly grasped how bullheaded Gabriella could be.

He was sure she was bluffing—maybe. Either way, he wasn't about to leave her side. He opened the door and got one leg out before Joaquin spoke.

"I will drive you." He sounded as if he had a gun jammed in his back. Maybe that's how he felt.

"To Chance's home?" Maybe Gabriella was less a bull and more a pit bull, because she wasn't about to let this go.

"Sí," the big man sighed wearily, as if the fifteen-mile-drive was a death march.

"Thank you." Gabriella pulled Chance back into the vehicle and slid her hand down his inner thigh.

And just like that, he didn't give a damn for what Joaquin might do tomorrow.

The pain of keeping his hands to himself was a new kind of hell, but soon enough the vehicle lurched to a sudden halt. Both of them startled. Chance saw they were at his house. Thank God for that.

He got out of the car, finally. Walking wasn't going to be the easiest thing he'd ever done, but he'd manage somehow.

Gabriella started to get out with him, but then she stopped. "My shoes…"

"You don't need them." He pulled her out and into his arms. "I'll carry you."

"Oh," she breathed, her eyes glazed over with desire. Then she tucked her head against his neck and kissed him there. His knees shook. "If you insist."

"I do." He turned toward the door and saw Joaquin standing next to it, looking as pissed as he possibly could. Chance didn't think issuing orders would go over real well, but he was sick to death of tiptoeing around the big man. "Will you keep an eye on the house? I don't want anyone to try to barge in on us." Including Joaquin.

"Please," Gabriella added.

Joaquin nodded—a swift, curt movement of his head. But he stepped aside.

Finally. Chance took the steps as fast as he could; took the hallway back to his room faster. He couldn't wait to pick up right where he'd left off in the car—with Gabriella holding on to her composure by the thinnest of threads.

He sat her on the bed, where she peeled off her jacket as he kicked off his shoes. Maybe later there'd be time for nice and slow. But the backseat tonight—hell, the front seat last night—had him primed. And, given the way she grabbed at his belt, she was rarin' to go, too.

But he didn't want to go *that* fast. Yeah, he was hard up—very hard up—but he wasn't the kind of man who took without giving anything back. So he grabbed her hands and held them away from his groin. "Slow down, woman."

"I don't want to slow down." She tested his grip on her. "I've waited for this for so long… I don't want to wait a moment longer."

He grinned as he pushed her back on the bed. Then he took the kiss on her lips she had waiting for him as he let his body settle over hers. "I want to do this right, Gabriella. Slow can be just as good as fast." To emphasize his point, he ground his hips into hers and was rewarded with a low moan of pleasure. "Slow can be better."

"All right. But I still want to see you." She pulled her hands free and began working at the buttons on his shirt. "Please."

"All you had to do was ask." He sat back and let her get the shirt undone, but then he stood and shucked both the shirt and jacket together before taking care of his pants himself. He couldn't have her touching him right now, not until he got himself a little more under control.

"Your turn." He knelt on the bed and lifted her hair away from her neck. Then he undid the tie of her top and let it fall forward.

He expected her to touch him while he did this, but she didn't. She sat there. Was she trembling? "If you want me to stop…" he offered, trying to sound as sincere as possible. If she'd changed her mind, he'd respect that. Even if it killed him.

"No! I want this. You." Then she swallowed.

She was nervous, he realized—but he wasn't sure why. Maybe she'd never had someone as big as him? And if not, should he take that as a compliment?

He leaned back, taking the time to admire her breasts. Even then, he couldn't help but notice that her gaze was locked onto his erection. "You are *so* beautiful," he told her as he cupped her chin in his hand and lifted her face up to his.

Then he stepped back and pulled her to her feet. He unzipped the skirt and let it fall with a swish to the ground. He filled his hands with the creamy skin of her hips—not the stick-thin hips of a woman who starved herself to fit some crazy notion of beauty, but the full, glorious hips of a woman. "So beautiful," he repeated as he slid his hands underneath her silky panties and slid them off.

Then there was nothing left between them. He pressed his lips against the base of her neck and felt the crazy-fast speed of her pulse. "You okay?" But he asked this as he ran his tongue over her the edge of her earlobe.

"I… It's…too slow. I want to go faster."

This pulled him up short. "Why?" Maybe she liked it fast? After all, she'd gone from zero to sixty in about 1.3 seconds last night in his truck.

She looked down at his straining erection and then, with a hesitant hand, reached out and touched him. Just the tip of her finger brushing the tip of his penis. As if she was afraid of it.

As if she'd never done this.

It hit him like a bolt out of the blue. "Gabriella, have you ever been with a man before?"

Before he could process this—she was a *virgin?*—she took him firmly in hand and stroked. It wasn't a particularly skilled stroke, but he was already so worked up that it temporarily short-circuited his brain.

"That…that does not matter, does it? You have, haven't you?"

Hell *yes,* it mattered. It mattered a lot. He hadn't been with a virgin since back when *he'd* been a virgin. Even at seventeen, the sex had been so awkward, so mind-bogglingly *bad* that his girlfriend had pretty much dumped him and he hadn't been all that sad to see her go. It was one of his least favorite memories involving the opposite sex. Hell, it *was* his least favorite one.

He'd gotten better, of course. Practice made perfect and he had a couple of lady friends who'd taught him the finer points of pleasing a female. At thirty-two, he'd gotten quite good.

But still…she was a virgin. At twenty-seven. It boggled his mind.

"Maybe we shouldn't do this." Being the first was a big responsibility. Bigger, given how long she'd waited.

"No!" Her head shot up, nearly clipping him in the chin. "No. I want this."

She gracefully fell to her knees. He knew what she was about to do—push him past the point of reason—and he tried to stop it, but the woman was hell-bent on changing his mind for him.

Her hands still trembling, she knelt in front of him. "I understand the process," she said, her voice flashing between confident and nervous. "I…have been told that it will not hurt because I spend so much time riding." Then she leaned forward and pressed those beautiful lips to his tip. "Do not deny me this, Chance. Please."

Then she took him in her mouth and it was all he could do to keep steady. Yeah, he'd say she had a pretty good grasp on "the process," as she'd put it. She swirled her tongue around him, one hand on his base, one hand wrapped around his leg for balance.

Had she ever done this—go down on someone? No, he didn't think so. She was too hesitant and, yes, too awkward to send him over the edge, but he didn't care. A twenty-seven-year-old virgin.

Anyone but him.

He looked down at Gabriella, doing her level best to seduce him. This was going to be tricky. How could he make it worth it for her—while also making sure she didn't feel like a failure of a woman for being inexperienced?

"Please," she said, pausing to catch her breath. She leaned her head against his thigh and traced his length with her fingertips. "*Please,* Chance. Do not treat me like a china doll that must be locked away. Treat me like a woman. I can see how much you want me." She stroked him again, making him twitch. "Can't you see how much I want you?" Then she took him in her mouth again.

Treat her like a woman who raced horses and looked as beautiful in a welder's apron as she did in a backless top and skirt.

He stroked her hair as she tried to time her hand movements to her mouth at a rate of speed that wasn't going to do anything but lead to inappropriate chafing. "Slow." He managed to get the word out through gritted teeth. "Go slow. Let me watch you."

Then she looked up at him, her eyes wide as her lips encircled him. The look in her eyes—*damn.* So innocent, so sexual at the same time. Desperate for him, for his approval. It was like a punch to the gut.

And she slowed way, *way* down. She was licking him like he was an ice cream cone and she was going to devour him one bite at a time.

Oh, yeah—she'd managed to push him past the point

of reason. "Yeah," he groaned as she licked him up and down again. "Just like that—*yeah*."

She pulled away and kissed his thigh again. "That was good?"

"That was *great*."

She looked up at him, her face beaming with satisfaction. Thank heavens that had been the right thing to say. But when she made a move to go down on him again, he pulled her up. "My turn, beautiful."

Before he laid her out on the bed and took what she wanted him to have, he wrapped his arms around her and held her. "If something doesn't work, you tell me. Okay?"

She felt so damn good against his chest, her head resting almost on his shoulder. She fit against him. With him. Then she said, "I can do that?"

It broke his heart a little bit, that she would even question her right to have a say in her own pleasure.

Then he realized that he'd been questioning that very thing a matter of moments earlier. She knew what she wanted. She'd been brave enough to ask for it.

And he had told her all she had to do was ask—the answer would be yes.

"Yup." He backed her up to the bed and laid her out on it. "Something not working, something you want to try—just ask, babe."

She scooted farther back onto the bed, giving him plenty of room—and a hell of a view of her luscious body. "All right."

"Do you want me to do to you what you did to me?" He'd been with a few women who weren't comfortable with oral sex. As much as he wanted to taste her—*all* of her—he felt it was only right to ask.

Her sensual smile stiffened. "I think...maybe it would be better to...you know...first."

Yeah, he'd guessed right on that one. She may have convinced him, but she was still nervous. "Maybe later?"

That got him a wicked grin. "Perhaps."

He leaned over and snagged a condom from the bed-side table. She watched as he rolled it on. Then he covered her body with his. She tensed, as if she expected him to plunge into the gap, but he didn't. He focused on relax-ing her—he ran his tongue over her dark nipples, blow-ing on them to make them tighten up. And to listen to her gasp in surprise.

"Good?"

"Oh, yes."

"Good." He worked his way up her chest to her neck, where he kissed and sucked while fondling her breasts until she was right where she'd been in the backseat of the car—bucking against him, her body begging for his. The whole time, her hands moved over his back—testing the muscles, digging into his skin when he did something she particularly liked.

He reached down between her legs and skimmed his hand over the glossy hair that covered her there. Untrimmed, untamed—just her in her natural state. He stroked her sex, feeling the tremors that shook her. "Good?"

"Ah, Chance," was the response he got, low and throaty in his ear.

He slipped one finger inside her. When her muscles clamped down on him, he about lost it then and there. But he focused on her, kissing her as she moaned at his touch.

He couldn't take it anymore. He was doing his damned-est to put her first, but he needed the release that was pounding in his blood. He needed her more than he'd ever needed any other woman.

He had to do this right.

Thirteen

Gabriella was having trouble breathing. Chance was doing things to her—things that she'd read about, *dreamed* about—but nothing had prepared her for the way his touch affected her.

She'd touched herself. She was only human, after all. She'd been about fifteen when she'd discovered that rubbing herself felt good and, if she kept doing it, it then felt great. Chance was rubbing her in that manner and it did feel good.

But he was inside her, too—and that was so much *more* than she'd expected. What was she supposed to be feeling? What if she wasn't doing this right? She'd basically thrown herself at his feet in such a scandalous way that she still couldn't believe she'd taken him into her mouth.

Then he pulled back. "You're so beautiful," he said in a voice that set her shaking again. Then, leaning back on one hand, he fitted himself against her and began to push.

Again, she wasn't sure what to expect. In books, a man often sank himself into his woman, an action that was quick and decisive and always painted as being very manly, even if it did mean that the woman hurt more because of it.

Chance did not do that. He moved slowly and paused

often. All the while, he kept kissing her lips, her neck, her shoulders. Then he would push forward again.

It didn't hurt. Thank heavens. It wasn't entirely comfortable, but she'd read about the pain of the quick tearing that went with this. No pain, no tearing.

Finally, Chance was fully inside her. "Doing okay?" he asked.

None of this was what she'd thought. She didn't even know the right way to respond to that thoughtful question. "I…um…yes?" She hadn't meant for it to come out as a question. She was sure there was nothing appealing about a woman who didn't have the first clue what she was doing in bed.

But instead of laughing or mocking her, Chance took a deep breath. As he did so, his hips moved—not a big gesture, but enough that she felt it deep inside. "You feel *so* good," he said, his voice little better than a whisper.

"Do I?"

"Oh, yeah." Then he flashed the crooked grin at her that made her forget all about what she may or may not supposed to be doing. All she could think of was being here, right now, with Chance. "Now for the fun part."

Oh, thank goodness—this hadn't been the fun part. Well, some of it had been fun, but she didn't yet see what everyone always made such a fuss about.

Then he moved. He pulled back and thrust forward, and then he did it again. Not the frenzied pace or hip-slamming often seen in movies—not that. This was slow, as he'd promised. It didn't hurt. His body covered hers, her body covered his and then—

Then he shifted a little and thrust in again and her world changed.

"Oh!" she gasped as the sensation went from *more* to *not enough* in a heartbeat. His body tapped hers with exquisite precision—a craftsman hammering a fine piece of gold—and suddenly her body rang with sensation.

It was as if he was the artist and she was the medium. He lifted her arms over her head and caught one of her nipples in his mouth as he rotated his hips into hers. Then he slid his hands under her bottom and guided her to wrap her legs around his waist. She moved the way he wanted her to, trusting that he would make this everything she'd hoped for. Better than she'd hoped for.

"You feel amazing," he said in that low voice that made her want to melt.

"Yes." Her body seemed to have developed a mind of its own. Instead of him moving her legs or arms, she was moving them herself—touching him however she could. Instead of him rotating his hips against her, she was swaying against him, testing the ways he filled her.

"Yeah, like that," he grunted in approval. "Does that feel good?"

"Yes." And it did. But… "I need more."

"All you had to do was ask." Chance pushed back onto his heels and pulled her bottom against him at a new angle. Then, as he began to thrust with a renewed vigor, he licked his fingertips and pressed them against her sex.

"Oh. *Oh!*" Overwhelmed with the pleasure that was both outside and inside her, she struggled to find something to hold on to. He was sitting too far back for her to reach him, let alone kiss him. She had to content herself with grabbing his forearm. But even that wasn't enough. As the pleasure built to heights she'd never dreamed of reaching by herself, she realized she was thrashing in the bed. It didn't seem dignified. But she was powerless to stop as long as he held her captive with his touch.

"Come on, babe." He spoke through gritted teeth. "So. Beautiful. Come for me."

She wanted to—oh, how she wanted to—but instead

of pushing her over the edge, his words called her back to herself. What if she couldn't come? Would he be insulted that he hadn't succeeded?

As these thoughts swirled around her desire, he leaned forward—without taking his fingers off her sex—and pried one of her hands from his arm. "Show me what you need."

Was he serious?

Oh, yes—he was quite serious. With his gaze locked onto hers, he ran his tongue over the tips of her fingers. Then he guided her hand down. "Show me," he said, half begging and half ordering.

So she did. She pressed against her most sensitive spot—his fingertips covering hers—and rubbed in the way that had always worked before.

Heat flooded her body as he held the eye contact. "So beautiful," he groaned before his body crashed into hers. He roared, a deep sound that did something to her—something she couldn't explain. He wasn't holding back, wasn't being calm and all-knowing—none of that.

She was doing that to *him*.

She didn't know if she pressed harder or if it was him or if they both did—but her body seized up and unleashed a climax upon her unlike anything she'd ever experienced before. Her body curled up on his, her back coming all the way off the bed as she shook around him—a work of art they'd made together.

The next thing she knew, Chance's arms were wrapped around her as he lowered her back onto the bed. "Did it hurt?" he asked, his voice concerned as he pulled free—but didn't let her go.

"What? No—it was—it was—" That was when she realized she was crying.

Oh, no. She was crying. In his bed.

This was the most embarrassing thing that had ever happened to her.

She ducked her head against his shoulder, too ashamed to look him in the eye. Chance chuckled and for the life of her, she couldn't tell if he was laughing at her or not. "It was...good?"

She nodded against his chest, thankful he couldn't see her stupid tears. Why was she crying? It had been the most wonderful thing that she'd ever felt! It was exactly what she'd wanted, exactly what she'd saved herself for all these years! Chance had put her needs first—he hadn't treated her like some fragile thing he was afraid to touch, nor had he treated her as a disposable woman like some girls on staff sometimes complained about.

"Was that the first time that happened?"

She nodded, trying in vain to get her emotions under control. Oh, this was not a sexy, sophisticated response. She was a blubbering idiot.

This realization only made things worse.

Chance pulled back and lifted her chin until she had no choice but to look at him. "You were amazing, you know? I'm so glad you came. I've never seen anyone as beautiful as you were. As you are."

"But...I'm a mess."

He grinned at her, but it wasn't the cocky grin that made her blood run hot. This grin made her feel safe in his arms, as if it were okay if she was sobbing in his bed. "You're not a mess. You're a woman. The one I'm in love with."

"Oh." And just like that, she no longer felt like an idiot, blubbering or otherwise.

She felt like she'd come home.

"I wish you could stay the night."

Gabriella had climbed back into his bed after they'd both taken a moment to clean up. She was curled into him underneath the covers, her body pressed against his.

Part of him wanted her to fall asleep because if she fell asleep, she'd stay.

He knew that wasn't going to happen. This moment was just that—a moment. One that would be too short.

"I wish I could, as well." As she spoke, she traced a path on his chest. Dang if her touch—light and sweet and hot all at the same time—didn't make him want to break out in goose bumps.

"We don't have much time, do we?"

She'd been a virgin who'd given herself to him. And it'd either been really bad or... He'd made her cry. That was a first for him. He'd been terrified that he'd hurt her but he didn't think she could lie about something like that. Instead, her emotions had been laid bare for him. As she'd been.

He still couldn't wrap his head around the whole thing, so he wrapped his arms around her instead.

Gabriella sighed against his chest, holding tighter to him. "No, we do not have much time." She sounded so sad about it.

He realized she was answering a different question— one that had nothing to do with tonight and everything to do with tomorrow. Or the next day. Or—if he were lucky—next month.

Suddenly he was talking without being entirely sure of what he was saying. "Whatever you want—that's what I'll do, babe. We can find a way to make this work. My door is always open to you or I'll come see you—all you have to do is ask and I'll be there."

She didn't say anything for a long moment. Instead she pressed her hand flat against his chest, right over his heart. "I want..." She trailed off, as though she didn't know how to actually say the words.

He leaned over to kiss her forehead, but he didn't rush

into the gap. She could ask him for anything. He had to make sure she knew that.

"I want to be with you as long as I can." Her voice was barely a whisper against his skin.

Because there'd come a time when she couldn't—when her path and his would stop crossing. When she'd stop defying Joaquin and, by extension, her father.

"Let's start with tomorrow. One day at a time. What do you want to do?"

She went back to tracing his skin again. It took a heck of a lot of effort to not roll into her, to not feel her body moving beneath his again.

"It might be…suspicious if we spent another evening together."

He ran through his schedule. The time between Valentine's Day and Mother's Day was pretty slow for him. He had a meeting with an ad firm in Houston to talk about commercials, but that was next week. Not tomorrow. "Luckily, I've got all day. Can you come out to work in the shop?"

"I believe so."

That was not the confidence-inspiring answer he was looking for, but he knew it was as good as it got. "You come out to work in the shop and I'll have lunch here for us." Franny would pack him up some sandwiches. If he was lucky, she might even do it without commentary.

"Just lunch?" He didn't have to look at her to know that she was smiling in that sly way of hers.

"I've got all afternoon, babe."

"Yes." She hummed against him. "*That* is what I want."

"Good." Even as he said it, he heard the sounds of heavy footsteps pacing downstairs. Joaquin was getting impatient, no doubt. They didn't have very long at all.

So he kissed her again, praying he'd see her right back here again tomorrow. "Because that's what I want, too."

* * *

For three days—three of the best days in Chance's memory—they got what they wanted. He met Gabriella at the barn in the morning where, after some not-so-quick kissing in the tack room, they'd mount up and race out to the shop. He'd kiss her goodbye for the morning and tend to the business of the ranch before he picked up lunch. They'd ride back to his house, have the kind of sex that got better every single time and eventually get around to reheating Franny's lunch.

Eventually.

The more time they spent together, the more comfortable Gabriella seemed to get about asking for what she wanted. She may have been a virgin, but she'd *thought* about sex a great deal. True, she couldn't meet his eyes when she asked if they could make love with him behind, but she'd asked. That was the important point. That and the explosive sex.

She also asked if they could have another picnic—and do it outside. Chance's first reaction was that it wasn't warm enough—they should wait for the weather to turn—but then he remembered their time was short. So he packed a couple of blankets and they kept most of their clothes on.

The more love they made, the more Chance wanted to make love with her. Even though they had sex every day, he still went to sleep with a hard-on that led to crazy dreams—dreams where Gabriella was sometimes older, sometimes with a baby on her hip, sometimes holding a red-hot spike and wearing a welder's mask. Every time, though, she'd look up at him through those thick lashes and say, "I want…" Even in his dreams, he did whatever he could to give her what she wanted.

Man, he was so gone. So damn *gone*.

Of course, he still had to deal with Joaquin, damn him. Franny always packed a double helping of the day's special for the big man. Joaquin stayed downstairs when Chance and Gabriella were upstairs and the day they had the picnic sex, he mounted up on Beast and rode a perimeter around them—far enough away that he couldn't hear moans, but close enough that he could hear the screams of terror he seemed to be expecting constantly.

Saturday rolled around. Slim didn't work on the weekends, so there was no good reason to justify Gabriella coming out to the ranch bright and early. Plus, she'd said she'd thought Alex might be feeling a little better and she wanted to spend some time with him. How was he supposed to begrudge her that?

They were going to give Claire's another go tonight to see if they could make it through a meal before he started peeling her clothes off her. The plan was that Gabriella would come out around five.

That didn't explain why Chance was showered and shaved by three-thirty, which left him an hour and a half of staring at the clock. Great.

He emailed a couple of clients about their upcoming events at McDaniel's Acres, thought about how he wanted his commercials to go—and kept staring at the clock. The minutes refused to tick by at any normal speed, damn them.

Finally he heard a car door slam outside. *Thank God.* He hurried to get the front door open for her. They had some time before their dinner reservations. Maybe she'd tell him something else she wanted, something they could do right now. Yeah, that'd be—

"Chance?"

As he swung the door open, he pulled up short. It wasn't Gabriella rushing to throw her arms around him—it was his old flame, Cara Windsor. And she was crying.

Aw, hell.

"Cara?" he asked as she clung to him. "What's wrong,

honey?" She'd been coming to him a lot, complaining about how Alex didn't remember her. It was hard to be sympathetic. Part of him didn't want to know. Part of him—a small part, but it was still there—wanted to let her twist in the wind for choosing a lying, cheating bastard over him.

"Oh, I'm so sorry—I didn't know where else to go. I don't know who else I can trust."

At least, that's what Chance thought she said. It was sort of hard to tell, what with the sobbing.

"Slow down, honey." Yeah, that small part of him might be happy watching her twist, but he pushed it back. They'd parted as friends—and she obviously needed a friend. He patted her on the back. "Tell me what's wrong."

"It's—" She didn't get very far before she buried her head on his shoulder.

Hell, not again. Chance managed to kick the door shut and guide her over to his couch. "There, there," he said, rubbing her back as she cried her eyes out. It probably wasn't the best thing to say, but he didn't have any better ideas.

He'd known Cara for a long time. They'd been friends before they were lovers, then back to friends again and she'd been crying on his shoulder about Alex for weeks now. But this was different. He'd never seen her this upset, and that worried him.

When she finally seemed to have cried most of it out, he tried again. "What's wrong? Are you in trouble?"

She looked at him, her light blue eyes watery and red. "Yeah, you could say that."

It broke his heart, just a little. "Tell me what happened and I'll try to fix it."

"You can't." Her eyes started to leak again, but she didn't start crying. "I...I messed up, Chance. I messed up real bad."

"What happened?"

"You know how worried I was about him, when he went missing."

"I know," he said in his most patient voice.

"And you know I never thought you were behind it." She got that steely look in her eyes, which momentarily chased her sadness away. "I *know* you weren't."

"I sure do appreciate that, honey. What happened now?" Because if this was just rehashing the past—again—well, he had a date to go on.

"One of the times I went to see him and he didn't remember me…" She dropped her gaze, suddenly finding her manicure very interesting. "So I…I had sex with him. To see if that would help him. Remember me."

"O…kay." This was exactly the sort of information he did *not* need to know. Not now, not ever.

"And now…" She covered her mouth with her hand, as if the words were cutting her on their way out. "And now I'm pregnant." She started to sob again in earnest.

"Oh, honey." Chance put his arm around her shoulders. This was exactly the kind of mess he couldn't fix. Alex was barely feeling "better," according to Gabriella. Had he even remembered he'd loved Cara yet?

Damn that man all over again. Why had he come up here and thrown a monkey wrench in all of their lives? Because as god-awful as it had been being guilty until proved innocent in Alex's abduction, that was a temporary thing. Nothing like having a baby. *Nothing.*

"I don't know what to do." Cara wept, pretty much trashing his date shirt. "I didn't know who else to trust. What am I going to tell my daddy?"

Oh, hell. It's not as if there was any love lost between Chance and Paul Windsor—but even Chance could see that springing "pregnant with the amnesiac's baby" on the old man would be a bad idea.

So he tried to deal with first things first. "Have you seen a doctor?"

She shook her head against his shoulder.

"That needs to happen. You schedule an appointment and get all checked out and we'll go from there, okay?" He tilted her head up to his and stared into her watery eyes. "You take care of you and that baby first. We'll deal with the rest of it second."

She gave him a weak smile as she nodded. He'd thought he'd loved this woman once. Maybe he had, but it hadn't been the same thing he felt for Gabriella. What he and Cara had shared was closer to a relationship borne of comfort and familiarity instead of passion and love.

"You're a good man, Chance McDaniel." It came out sniffly. "I was afraid you might tell me I'd gotten exactly what I'd deserved for leaving you."

"I wouldn't do that." He meant it, too. He'd lost this woman, but maybe he'd never had her. Now that he had Gabriella—now that he had tasted true passion—he knew that it was for the best.

"I know. I knew I could trust you." She leaned up and pressed a kiss to his cheek.

A sharp gasp cut through the room, making him turn toward the now-open door—and the woman standing in it.

Oh, *hell*. Gabriella.

Her eyes cut between Chance and Cara at an alarming rate of speed. "Babe," he got out, trying to pull free of Cara's arms and stand all at the same time.

But before he could do any of that, she turned and marched right back out.

"Was that…Alex's sister?" Cara let him go, thank God.

He didn't answer. He flat-out ran to catch up with Gabriella, but he was too late. Joaquin was shutting the back door.

"It's not what it looked like," Chance said, putting his

life on the line to keep walking toward the car. "I need to talk to her."

Joaquin gave no sign that he'd heard Chance. "Joaquin! *¡Vámonos!*" came a muffled cry from the backseat.

Shit. She was already crying. "I need to talk to her," he demanded as he kept walking toward the car. "I didn't do anything."

Joaquin pulled his piece on Chance in one smooth motion, leveling the barrel at Chance's guts.

Cara appeared in the doorway. "What's going on?" Then she squeaked. "Chance! He's got a gun!"

He didn't take his eyes off the weapon. "Go inside, Cara. Joaquin, I'd never hurt her. Never. You know I wouldn't."

"Joaquin! *¡Llévame a casa ahora!*" Gabriella's voice was close to hysterical.

The weirdest thing happened. Joaquin's mouth opened and he said, "Stay away from her." He holstered his gun and walked around to the driver's side of the vehicle. With a final cutting look, the big man climbed in and peeled off, leaving Chance in a cloud of dust, wondering if he'd actually heard Joaquin talk.

He couldn't do anything but watch the vehicle disappear down the road at a high rate of speed. It felt as though his heart was being dragged along behind it, tied to the bumper. The pain almost doubled him over. He wanted to go after her—but he didn't want to die. Even if not going after her felt a little bit like dying anyway.

"Chance?" Cara came out and put a hand on his arm. "Are you okay? Did he shoot you? Do you want me to call Nathan?"

"No." Involving the local sheriff in this would only make everything a million times worse. Yeah, he could have Joaquin arrested—and yeah, he'd like to see the big man rot in jail for a couple of years—but what would that get him?

It wouldn't get him Gabriella. He knew damn good and well that he'd never see her again.

He *had* to see her again. If he could explain what had happened, this whole misunderstanding would melt into nothingness. Because that's what it was—nothing.

He'd explain that Cara was in a bit of trouble—that she'd come to him for advice, that was all. All she wanted from him was a shoulder to cry on. No one had been seducing anyone.

"That was Alex's sister, wasn't it? Oh, God, Chance. Did I mess something up?"

"No, honey. Just a misunderstanding." He patted her on the hand. "Something I've got to get cleared up."

"I didn't know that you were seeing her." Cara's eyes were watering with more vim and vigor now. "I'll go talk to her."

He couldn't see that going well, either. He'd seen Gabriella turn on Joaquin enough to know she had a lot of fight in her. What would she do to Cara? "Let me handle this. Her bodyguard is a mean sucker. I don't want you in harm's way, okay? You focus on you, Cara. You and your baby. Let me worry about this."

She gave him that weak smile. "Will you tell Alex? About me? And the baby?"

"That's not my place, honey."

They stood there in pained silence for a moment, watching the cloud of dust stirred up by Joaquin's driving settle back over the land. Before long, there wouldn't be any sign that they'd been here at all. The land had a way of doing that—taking whatever it'd seen and returning it to the dirt. The land had taken in all of his family, his hopes for a family of his own, all of his blood, sweat and tears. It would continue on long after he'd left.

No. He wouldn't let his feeling for Gabriella settle. This wasn't over. He wasn't going to let Gabriella go without a fight the way he'd let Cara go.

He had to go after her.

Fourteen

By the time Chance got Cara on her way with the promise to call her doctor first thing Monday morning, almost forty minutes had passed. Damn it all.

He didn't have much of anything that resembled a plan, beyond finding Gabriella. That was it. It would have to be enough. It had to be. He wasn't going to let it end this way. Maybe it would end, sooner or later, but to have her think he'd been cheating? To have her think he didn't love her? Nope. Not happening. She could still end it, but she was going to know the truth of the matter.

So when Alex del Toro's red Ferrari went zooming past him on a deserted road at the edge of Royal, Chance slammed on the brakes. All he could think was, *Alex?*

Alex had clearly thought the same thing—he'd turned his Ferrari around and pulled up behind Chance's truck.

Both of them got out at the same time. "Alex?" Chance said first. "Man, where have you—"

That was as far as he got before Alex reared back and punched him. Pain exploding around his eye, Chance stumbled to the side, barely managing to keep his feet under him. "What the hell, man?"

"Stand up so I can punch you again, McDaniel," Alex growled.

"Not without a damn good reason," Chance replied, blinking through the pain. He did stand, but he made sure it was out of swinging range.

Then he realized that Alex called him McDaniel—just as he's always said it after Chance had beaten him in a race out to the swimming hole. "You know who I am?"

"Of course I know who you are, you ass. You broke my sister's heart." Alex took a few quick steps, his fist balled up and ready to swing.

"Damn it, knock it off! I didn't break anyone's heart!" Chance sidestepped his *former* friend. He didn't want to hit the man with amnesia. If he still had it.

He caught Alex's arm on the swing-through and pushed, backing him into his Ferrari door. "Who was she?" Alex sneered. "A guest? Or an old girlfriend?"

He charged again. Chance had no choice. He ducked down and caught Alex around the waist. This time, it wasn't a defensive push. This time, Chance slammed Alex into the side of his car with enough force that the man groaned.

But he let go and stood back. "Shut up and listen, you idiot. It *was* an old girlfriend—Cara Windsor. Remember her? You stole her from me and she fell in love with you."

"Cara?" Oh, yeah—the way Alex hissed that? He knew exactly who Cara was. "You're screwing around on my sister with *Cara?* I'm going to kill you, McDaniel."

"The hell you are. Shut up and listen for a moment."

"To what? You explain how you made a move on my woman while I was sick?"

"Yeah, because you're so damn sick right now you can hardly throw a punch." He touched the side of his face, which was already swelling. But, miracle of miracles, Alex didn't charge him again.

"Fine. You have two minutes."

Chance took a breath, hoping that would help his now

throbbing head. It didn't. He'd promised Cara not an hour ago that he wouldn't tell Alex about her and the baby—Alex's baby. But he couldn't have the man thinking Chance would step out on Gabriella.

"Think, man—why would Cara come crying on my shoulder? Because that's what she was doing—crying to me because she's been worried sick about *you,* you lying, thieving bastard." There. That was almost the truth. Cara had been worried for weeks and she'd probably been feeling sick. Alex was the root cause of both problems. Not a lie.

Plus, it felt damn good to call Alex out. "Or do you believe the same lies about me that everyone else believes? That I kidnapped you to win her back? No, wait—I forgot. The only liar here is you, *Alejandro.*"

"Don't call me that," he replied in a low voice.

"Why not? It's your name, isn't it?"

"Not anymore."

Chance threw his hands up. "And I'm supposed to take you at your word, right? Because you've never lied to me? You've always been an up-front guy? *Wrong.* Hell, I don't know who you are or why you came to Texas. All I know is that, by being your friend, you screwed my life up pretty damn bad and that I'm in love with your sister."

He hadn't actually meant to say that last part about Gabriella, but he'd built up a head of steam and it had slipped out.

The two of them stood there for a moment, the shock of Chance's words tripping them both up.

When Alex didn't take another swing at him, Chance hung his head. "Look—I don't know who you are or why you strung me along for close to a year. And right now, I don't much care. I'm going to go talk to Gabriella. I would never hurt her and I sure as hell would never cheat on her."

He turned and started walking back to his truck.

"Wait," Alex called out behind him. "Joaquin will kill you. I'm surprised he didn't earlier."

Yeah, that made two of them. He looked back over his shoulder at Alex. "If it's all the same to you, I'll risk it."

"No," Alex said again. He moved, but instead of throwing another punch, he grabbed Chance's arm. "It would destroy her."

Chance turned to look at Alex—a hard look. The man dropped his hand from Chance's arm. "Oh, so you remember who she is now?"

Alex couldn't meet his eyes. "She is my sister. I would do anything to protect her."

Suddenly, Chance had the urge to deck Alex and it had nothing to do with the black eye he was working on. "Stop protecting her, for God's sake. She's a grown woman. Let her do whatever the hell she wants. That's *all* she wants, you know."

"Let me talk to her," Alex went on, almost as if Chance hadn't spoken. "She's upset. She said she saw another woman kiss you. She's never had her heart broken before." He looked up at Chance but instead of his earlier rage, he was more confused this time. And less violent. "Was Cara kissing you?"

"On the cheek, damn it!" He grabbed the collar of his shirt, still messed up from Cara's crying, and held it out for Alex to see. "The literal shoulder to cry on! And what the hell are you doing out here, worried about your sister? Do you have any idea how *worried* Cara is about you? How 'seducing' me is the very last damn thing she's thinking of? How, even if there was a shot in hell that she was trying to seduce me I'd never let it get that far because, unlike *some* people, I respect my friends." Alex had the freaking nerve to look wounded by this statement, which only made Chance madder. "Mind your own damn business, Alex, and for the love of everything holy, let me mind mine!"

He turned and stomped off toward his truck, wrenching the door open with more force than was technically necessary.

"Joaquin *will* kill you if you show up at my house," Alex called after him.

"I'm not letting her go. Not like this," Chance called back, one foot in the truck.

"Let me talk to her. I owe you that."

Chance glared at the man. "You owe me a crap-ton more than that, *amigo*. Or did I forget to mention that the whole town thinks I tried to kill you?"

Alex had the decency to look ashamed at this. "Let me talk to her. I'll tell her what happened. She needs to calm down—once she calms down, Joaquin will calm down."

Chance didn't move. *He* wanted to be the one to talk to Gabriella, but…Joaquin *would* kill him without blinking an eye. "And you expect me to take you at your word like the same old sucker, huh? Fool me once, shame on you. Fool me twice, shame on me."

Now it was Alex's turn to hang his head. "I do not want your blood on my hands, Chance." He looked up and Chance thought he saw something honest in the man's eyes. "You have always been and will always be my friend. That part was real."

Or was it another lie, added to a pile of lies? "I don't believe you."

"Believe this—I've never seen Gabriella as happy as she is when she comes back from her time with you. It's like… it's like she's become the woman she always wanted to be but never had the courage to try before. I know what our father's like—I've tried so hard to step out of his shadow… She never had the chance. Until she met you."

Damn it, was Chance going to fall for this line of bull?

Yeah, he was. Because he could see the truth of the words. Rodrigo del Toro was a monster of a man. Plus,

Gabriella had said as much—when she was with him, she was the woman she wanted to be. He'd believed her then.

He believed Alex now.

"You screw me over again and we won't have to worry about Joaquin. Do I make myself clear?"

Alex sighed, looking as if that was what he'd expected, but somehow it was still disappointing. "Crystal. I'll call you tomorrow. We'll have to work around my father. Hopefully, she can get out for dinner. Is that okay?"

No. But what other plan did he have? He didn't trust Alex but he believed Joaquin would shoot him and it would destroy Gabriella. Besides, he didn't particularly want to die today. Or tomorrow, for that matter.

So, against his better judgment, he put his faith in the one man who didn't deserve it—Alex del Toro.

"Yeah, call me tomorrow."

"I will," Alex promised.

"You damn well better."

"That was Cara? *Windsor?*" Gabriella couldn't get her head around it. The woman Chance was rumored to have kidnapped Alex for was the one in his arms? On his couch?

"Yes." Alex looked terrible, but it wasn't the same kind of terrible that he'd been faking for weeks. This time, Gabriella thought he looked…guilty.

"But they weren't kissing. He was just comforting her? Because she was—what? Upset about you?"

"Yes," Alex repeated, looking even more miserable.

"And this was all one giant misunderstanding, was it?" At least they were alone. Joaquin had not followed her into her room when she'd rushed into the house and thrown herself on her bed in a truly melodramatic fashion. For that she was grateful. She could only hope he had not returned to McDaniel's Acres to finish Chance off.

"Yes."

Gabriella's cheeks burned, but she couldn't tell if that was out of relief or embarrassment. When she'd seen Chance with his arms around that blond woman, she'd experienced a shock so physical that it had been all she could do not to lose her stomach's contents right then and there.

Chance had said he'd loved her. And he'd been holding another woman.

All she'd been able to think was that she'd been a fool. She'd saved herself, and for what? She was just as disposable as all the maids had complained about during her youth. Disposable and replaceable.

She'd been the same fool her brother had been; falling for the sweet words of a man who would *always* betray the del Toro family at the first available moment.

But here sat Alex, protesting that she had somehow *not* seen what she'd seen, that Chance had not been wooing another woman. She didn't know if she should be happy that Chance was as trustworthy as she believed him to be or embarrassed that she hadn't trusted him even more.

She didn't want to see Chance just yet, not until she could sort through all the conflicting feelings that were making breathing a difficult chore. And Alex, despite his earnest intentions, had not seen what she'd seen.

Which meant there was only one other person she could ask.

"Where is your phone?"

"What?" Alex gave her an odd look, but he dug it out of his pocket. "Why?"

"I do not have Cara Windsor's number. You do. Call her. I want to speak to this woman."

He paled. "I don't know if that's a good idea…"

A flash of anger pushed back against her confused relief. "You do not think *what* is a good idea? Me, talking to another woman? Me, attempting to resolve a problem on my own? Me, being responsible for my own fate? I want to talk to Cara. If you do not give me her number, I will find another way to get it. And I will not hesitate to tell everyone in this three-horse town that your mind is as solid as it was the day you came north of the border!"

Alex gaped at her in shock, as if she had never spoken to him in such a way. Perhaps she hadn't, but she was sick to death of her family smothering her. She wanted to breathe without having to account to someone for her need of oxygen.

Then his mouth quirked up into a smile as he began tapping his screen. "A *two*-horse town. Not three. Didn't Chance teach you anything?"

"He taught me *many* things," she retorted. She couldn't even blush when he shot her a surprised look. She held out her hand for the phone.

"Should have let Joaquin shoot him," he muttered as he handed the ringing phone over.

"Alex? Baby, is that you? Oh, thank God!" The woman's voice on the other end of the phone spoke so fast that Gabriella had trouble understanding her. "Baby, I've been so worried about you—when can I see you?"

This Cara did not sound particularly guilty about being caught kissing Chance. If anything, she sounded as though she was crying.

"Ah, hello? This is Gabriella del Toro. Alex's sister." She looked at Alex, who had leaned in close to listen to the conversation. She couldn't decipher the look on his face, though.

"Oh." This momentary disappointment was quickly erased by concern. "Is he all right? Is everything okay?"

"Alex is fine." Although Cara Windsor sounded somewhat hysterical, Gabriella couldn't say that was a bad thing. Her concern for Alex—and her lack of concern for Chance—was a good sign.

But emotions were easy to fake over the phone. "I think

there may have been a misunderstanding earlier today. I'd like to meet you in person so we can get it cleared up."

"Chance would never cheat on you. I mean, he'd never cheat on anyone—he's not like that. This is all my fault…" She sounded as if she were crying again.

"Is there somewhere we could go for coffee to talk?"

"Do you…? Can I see Alex? Will he come with you?"

At this, Alex shook his head. "Ah, no. Not yet. But soon, I believe."

"All right." Cara sniffed. "We can meet at the Royal Diner—in an hour? Does that work for you?"

Gabriella looked at the clock. It was seven now. By eight, the dinner crowd of a diner should have cleared. Besides, she probably needed to fix her makeup and change into more appropriate clothing. Something far less revealing. "That would be fine. I'll see you then."

She ended the call and handed the phone back to her brother. "Thank you."

"Don't tell her I remember."

"Why not? She's obviously worried about you." Her frustration bubbled over. "I'm tired of living inside your deceptions, Alex. When will it all end?"

He took her hand then, patting it as if she was a small child again. Then he stood.

"Soon. I promise."

Perhaps she shouldn't be so disappointed by this small lie, not compared to all the rest. But she was.

She wished she could believe him.

Exactly an hour later Joaquin pulled up outside the Royal Diner. He was not happy about this excursion. Gabriella could tell by the way he would not meet her gaze, but she did not care.

Not when there was a chance that Chance had been honest with her. She had to know.

She recognized Cara immediately. The slim blonde was sitting in a booth at the back, dabbing at her eyes and staring at the coffee cup in front of her.

Gabriella did not want to do this. She was in no mood to offer up her heart just to have it ripped out of her chest for the second time today.

But she needed to know that Chance wouldn't have betrayed her. She needed to *believe* it.

"Cara?" When the woman looked up and gave her a sad smile, Gabriella slid into the booth. Joaquin took a spot at the counter, but he wasn't within earshot. Not if Gabriella kept her voice low.

A waitress immediately brought over a cup of coffee. "Anything else, hon?"

"We're fine, Amanda," Cara answered. "Thanks."

"Let me know." This Amanda gave Cara a quick squeeze on the shoulder before making her rounds to the other patrons of the diner.

"I suppose there's no good way to start, is there?" Cara sat back, her chin a little higher but her eyes still quite red. "I'd heard you were in town, but I didn't realize that you and Chance…"

She did not want to know what other people were "realizing" about her and Chance. So she hurried to cut Cara off.

"And I had only recently found out about you," Gabriella admitted.

"How is Alex? Does he…does he remember me?" Her eyes began to water again.

Gabriella felt a deep level of sympathy with this woman—a woman she would have been willing to throw to the wolves earlier today. She knew how painful it was when Alex wouldn't remember her. What if Chance suddenly didn't remember her? It would break her heart over and over again.

She chose her words carefully. "He is…improving." She couldn't say more, no matter how dishonest it was.

"Oh, that's good. That's better than…than—" Cara broke off, covering her mouth with her hand. "I'm glad you called," she went on when she had herself back under control. "I feel terrible about what happened this afternoon. I went to see Chance because, well, because I needed a friend and that's what Chance is—a friend. He's a wonderful man and it's been awful that people have been spreading lies about him, about how he hurt Alex to get me back. Chance isn't like that—he never has been. He cares for his friends—even when his friend dumped him for his best friend." Her face twisted into a mask of pain and guilt.

"I see," Gabriella said, wondering if she could trust this woman or if the weeping was all part of the act.

Cara must have heard the doubt in Gabriella's voice because she looked up and said, "I went to see Chance today because I'm pregnant with Alex's baby and he doesn't remember me. I…I don't know what to do."

"*¡Dios mío!*" Gabriella whispered, trying to process all the information Cara Windsor had just shared. Her brain tried to filter the fact that Alex would be a father in three different languages but all that happened was a hum of noise in her head. "A *baby?* Alex's baby?"

"When Alex's number came up on my phone, I was so excited— If I could tell him what's happened, maybe I could help him remember. I just want him to remember that he loved me."

Gabriella knew those feelings—weeks of being trapped in a house with a man who wasn't entirely her brother anymore and trying everything she could to help his memory. She felt for Cara Windsor. But she had to guard her own heart first. "There is nothing between you and Chance?"

Cara shook her head vigorously. "We're friends. We've always been friends. I think we'll always be friends—but nothing more. I love Alex Santiago." Her eyes began to water again. "The man I thought Alex was."

Gabriella could not help herself. She leaned forward and placed her hand on Cara's. "He loved you, too. I am certain of it. I believe he still does, but it's buried inside." That was not a lie, either. The only difference was that Alex was willfully keeping those emotions buried—it had nothing to do with head trauma.

"Thank you. Thank you for meeting me and letting me explain about Chance. I want him to be happy. He's a kind, sweet man and I tried so hard to love him. But then I met your brother..." She trailed off, looking lost in thought. "I asked Chance not to tell Alex I was expecting. I know we just met and you don't owe me a thing, but can I ask the same of you? I want to tell him face-to-face. Maybe it'll help."

Another lie. Gabriella tried very hard to keep the weariness off her face. Everyone had secrets that must be kept at all costs. Was she any different? She was in Chance's bed—something she did not want her father to find out under any circumstances.

And now this. A baby complicated things in ways that she had not dreamed were possible. What would Rodrigo del Toro do when he found out that his daughter was sleeping with a rancher and his son had fathered a child? She did not even want to contemplate the scene.

"No matter what, that baby is family, which makes you family." Gabriella felt herself tearing up as she spoke the words. "I won't tell Alex, but if there is anything I can do for you, do not hesitate to ask. The del Toro family has considerable resources at our disposal."

"The only thing I want is my Alex back," Cara said.

"We all do," Gabriella agreed. "We all do."

Fifteen

Chance slept fitfully with his phone in his hand, his boots by the side of the bed and an ice pack on his face. He knew that Gabriella wasn't going to call him at five in the morning to kiss and make up, but he couldn't help himself.

He had terrible dreams about Alex kicking him while he was down and Gabriella being pulled away from him.

He shouldn't have trusted the man, he decided as he made coffee at five-fifteen, his phone within easy reach on the counter. He should have risked being gut-shot by that damn guard so that he could be the one to talk to Gabriella. None of this second-hand horseshit. He didn't exactly know how the del Toro family operated—although he had a damn good idea—but the buck always stopped with the McDaniel men. He'd been comforting Cara. It should have been his job to make things right with Gabriella.

Six o'clock passed at slower than molasses in January. Seven did the same. By the time eight crawled by, Chance had drunk way too much coffee and was officially jittery.

Maybe he should go on over to the house. Hadn't that been a romantic movie back in the 80s? *Say...Something?* No, *Say Anything*—that'd been the movie where the guy stood on his car and blasted music from a boom box to wake up his girlfriend after a fight.

Chance went so far as to dig out his iPod before he realized he probably couldn't crank the volume loud enough for her to hear it in Alex's big house. Besides, the neighbors would probably call the cops on him. Nathan Battle, the sheriff, probably wouldn't arrest him, but it'd make a hell of a scene—and not the kind that would sway Gabriella to take him back.

Damn it all. He was going to drive himself insane in record time. If patience was a virtue, Chance was up to his eyeballs in sin right about now. How on God's green earth was he supposed to hold out until dinner tonight?

So when his phone rang at eight-thirty, he physically pounced on the damn thing in his eagerness to answer it. *Please be Gabriella,* he thought as he touched the screen, even though it was Alex's number. *Please be Gabriella.* "Hello?"

"Chance?"

At any point in the past few months, Chance would have been thrilled to hear his friend call him by name. Except for right now. "Yeah?"

"Tell me Gabriella is with you," Alex said, and Chance heard the panic in the man's voice.

"What do you mean? Of course she's not with me. I'm sitting here waiting for you to call and tell me everyone's calmed down. Where is she?"

"I don't know. She's not in her room and Joaquin says he hasn't seen her this morning."

"Have you searched the house?"

"I even checked the pool and the clubhouse—she's *gone.*"

Jesus, Alex was supposed to be calming her down—she wouldn't have done anything drastic, would she?

No. He didn't believe she'd do something like that. But that didn't mean something drastic hadn't happened.

"Check the damn house again. I'm coming over. Call Nathan."

"Papa doesn't want me to. We don't even know if she's missing. Chance—"

Hell, no. Alex wasn't going to pull the same line of bull about how he should handle this. This was exactly what Chance got for letting another man fight his battles. "I'm coming over." He hung up and dialed again. Carlotta answered at the front desk of the Bunk House. "Good morning, *señor.*"

"Carlotta, Gabriella has disappeared. We may have another kidnapping on our hands. Have the maids check every single room in the hotel, no exceptions. Wake up the whole damn place if you have to." He hung up and dialed a second time. "Marty? Gabriella's gone missing. Round up as many men as you can and start combing the range. Check Slim's shop first, the swimming hole second. Call me the moment you find her."

It was possible that she'd gone to those places—someplace quiet and familiar, where she could think.

But something told him that wasn't the case. What if the people who'd taken Alex had come for Gabriella? The thought made his stomach turn and turn hard. As much as she'd tried to keep a stiff upper lip when she'd told him about her mother's kidnapping and the attempts—both real and staged—on her life, he'd been able to tell that being taken was the scariest thing in her life.

God, he prayed as he drove at top speed, *keep her safe. Even if she's not mine to hold, keep her safe. Don't let her be scared.* Gabriella was a religious woman. Hopefully someone was answering prayers up there today.

She never went anywhere without Joaquin. Sometimes, after they'd made love and were lying in bed, she'd told him more about her life on her father's estate. She'd told him about a stable boy she'd kissed more out of defiance than love, about cutting off her hair when she was forbidden to go to "university," as she put it. She even told him about Raoul, the man her father allowed to escort her to events, and how he would put his hands on her as if he owned her. Which was why she'd never slept with him.

Never once had she mentioned actually sneaking out and giving old Joaquin a run for his money.

Something about this whole thing smelled worse than a cow patty in the summer sun.

He made it to Alex's house in record time. The place was quiet, like it was another regular Saturday morning. Obviously, Alex had not called the damn cops. Yet. What was wrong with that man?

He didn't bother with such crap as ringing a doorbell or knocking. He opened that door and walked right in to find Alex on the phone and Joaquin slumped down on the couch. Something was even more wrong than he thought.

"I got the maids checking the hotel and Marty checking the ranch," he said with no other introduction. "Where the hell is your father?"

Alex shot him a frantic look. "He's 'in a meeting' if you can believe that," Alex snapped before turning back to the phone. "Yes, I know—but I'd appreciate it if you could check. Thanks." He ended the call. "I've checked the pool and clubhouse again, gone through the house top to bottom. Nathan's going to start looking." Then, looking contrite, he added, "Sorry about your face."

The black eye Alex had given him was the least of his worries. "You actually called the sheriff?"

"Papa said not to, then locked himself in his office. Something's off and I don't like it."

"Yeah," Chance said, turning to the only other person in the room—the only person who wasn't frantic. "Yeah, something sure as hell seems off. Where is she?"

Joaquin didn't respond. Not in words, anyway. But he leaned forward and put his head in his hands.

Suddenly, Chance wished to holy hell that he'd brought his shotgun. Screw that. He could do a hell of a lot of damage without one.

He walked up to Joaquin, grabbed the man by the shirt and hauled him to his feet. That the big man didn't offer any resistance only confirmed Chance's suspicions. "Where the hell is she? You never let her out of your sight. For God's sake, you sit in my living room when we're in bed to make sure that no one bothers us."

"Man," Alex whispered. "I don't want to know that about my sister."

Joaquin dropped his eyes.

"I'd have thought," Chance said, ignoring Alex and giving Joaquin a little shake, "after *all this time,* you wanted her to be happy. That was why you let her be with me—it made her happy to ride and to work metal and to fall in love. But you never cared about her, did you? She was just some girl you had to watch. Just an *assignment* you had to complete. Tell me where she is, Joaquin, or you'll rot in hell for the rest of this eternity and the next."

The big man was silent, as if Chance had already broken him but hadn't realized it yet. "You know who took her and you let them do it," he yelled in Joaquin's face, hoping to get a reaction—any reaction—out of him. "You rat bastard, you *let* them do it."

"Correction," a stern voice with a thick accent announced from behind Chance. He let go of Joaquin, who dropped like a sack of potatoes, and spun to face Rodrigo del Toro. "He did not go with Gabriella because I ordered him not to."

"Another sick little test? You disgust me. The way you treat your daughter—*both* your children—is nothing short of criminal."

Chance realized too late that he was shouting at Gabriella's father, but he didn't care. This man—this monster—had done something with her and Chance *had* to get her back.

For his part, Rodrigo looked unmoved by Chance's insults. Instead he turned to Alex. "*This* is the man you befriended?" He looked to Joaquin. "*This* is the man you allowed my daughter to spend time with?" Both times, he spoke as if Chance were a piece of crap he'd stepped in. "I held you to a higher standard, Joaquin. I entrusted you with the thing that was most precious to me and you failed. Your services are no longer required by the del Toro family."

"Gabriella is *not* a thing," Chance growled. He'd never wanted to hit a man so hard in his entire life. One well-placed punch could take the older man down for good. "She's a woman. Where the hell is she?"

Not that Rodrigo was worried about getting punched. "When Joaquin told me of her involvement with a *rancher* like you, I knew I could not allow it to continue."

"What did you do, Papa?" Alex sounded as if his world was crumbling—and he couldn't do anything but watch it go. Why the hell wasn't he madder? Chance wondered. Why the hell wasn't he freaking *furious?*

"Raoul Viega came for her," Rodrigo said in a matter-of-fact tone. "Clearly, Gabriella is no longer happy at Las Cruces and, equally clearly, she is ready to be married. Raoul is from a suitable class. His father is a valuable business partner. This will cement our ties and Raoul will keep her safe."

"You—what? You *gave* her to Raoul?" Chance could not believe the words coming out of this man's mouth. Of all the bat-shit-crazy things he'd ever heard, treating your daughter like a party favor had to rank right up there.

"She is my daughter," Rodrigo replied in the haughtiest voice Chance had ever heard. "I will do with her as I see fit."

"The hell you will." Chance spun back to where Joaquin sat collapsed on the couch, looking for all the world as if he'd been shot and was bleeding out. "I'm hiring—head of security at McDaniel's Acres. New position—just opened up. You interested?"

"Qué?"

"He fired you. I'm hiring you. The first job I have for you is finding Gabriella. You in?"

Joaquin gaped at him, so Chance turned to Alex. "You in?"

"You would not dare," Rodrigo threatened. "Alejandro, you would not *dare* go against my direct orders."

Behind him, Chance felt Joaquin get to his feet. He braced for a blow, but what came next was an even bigger surprise. "They left half an hour ago. I know his car."

Rodrigo's face contorted with unmasked rage. "You will *suffer* for this, Joaquin."

Chance kept looking at Alex. Just yesterday, he'd told Chance that he knew what his father was like. Well, Chance did now, too. "You *in?* I can't wait around all day."

"Alejandro!" Rodrigo roared.

Alex dropped his head like a small boy who'd been beaten down one too many times. But then he lifted his head, his eyes lit with new fire. "My name," he said to his father as he began walking toward the door, "is Alex."

"Let's get gone," Chance said, clapping his old friend on the back and doing his level best to ignore the threats in both Spanish and English that followed the three men out of the house. He shut the door to block the older man out.

They had to get Gabriella before she made it south of the border. Even if she decided that he'd been nothing more than a great way to spend the time while she was stuck in Texas—even if she never wanted to see him again, he couldn't stand by while some entitled business brat took her home and married her.

"We've got a lot of road to cover. Call Nathan back and tell him what we know. Maybe one of his cop buddies can get their car stopped before they hit the border."

"Done. I'll follow you in my car." Alex was dialing before Joaquin got the car door shut.

"Keep up," was all Chance said. Then they were gone.

Sixteen

"I want," Gabriella said in the most level voice she could manage, "to go home."

Raoul snorted in the way that had always reminded her of a pig snuffling in its trough. "We'll be home soon enough. You will enjoy Casa Catalina. Your father will have your things sent over. You will want for nothing."

"I want," she repeated with a little more force, "to go back to Alex's house. Right *now*."

Raoul snorted again. Then he reached over and grabbed her thigh with more pressure than was comfortable. "You will grow to love Casa Catalina. You will grow to love *me*. We shall be married next week." And he squeezed her thigh hard enough to leave marks through the jeans she'd hurried into this morning, half-asleep when Joaquin had come into her room and told her to get dressed.

It hurt, but she refused to let a whimper of pain escape her lips. She would not let this man know that she was terrified of what he was saying. "When my papa finds out what you have done…" But even as she said it, she knew it was not the case.

"I'll have you know, *muñequita,* that he called me yesterday and told me to come get you. He said you weren't safe in America anymore."

Muñequita. Little doll. It was supposed to be a term of endearment, but it grated on her very last nerve. A little china doll to be locked behind glass, protected from everything. Protected from *life*. A doll was all she was to her father and that's all she was to Raoul.

With a final squeeze, Raoul took his hand off her leg.

Gabriella kept her mouth shut. Arguing was pointless. Obviously, Raoul would not be swayed from the path he and her father had agreed on. She was to be married within a week to this man, who would lock her up on a different estate and only touch her when he wanted to, not when she wanted him to. That, of course, would be never. The only man she wanted to touch her was Chance. Raoul may think he'd have an easy time of it now that she was no longer a virgin, but she would fight him every step of the way.

Starting now. What were her options? She could hit him with something. She had grabbed her purse on her way out to the garage, where Joaquin had said someone was waiting for her. She'd foolishly hoped it was Chance making some grand romantic gesture. Instead she'd found herself being roughly shoved into the open door of Raoul's Porsche. Joaquin had closed the door, narrowly missing her foot, and then Raoul had been backing out of the garage, locking the doors as he went.

Texas was a large state and, as far as she could tell, Raoul was obeying all traffic laws. He probably thought it prudent to avoid getting pulled over by a police officer. Soon, they would be near Midland, Texas—if she could only get out of the car, there was a chance she could find someone who would help her. She had her phone—surely a 9-1-1 call would bring the police?

If she hit Raoul, he might lose control of his car and wreck—which would kill them both.

For the first time in her life Gabriella understood how her mother must have felt when she'd been taken from the market so many years ago. Would Gabriella risk death to get back to the man she loved, as her mother had done to get back to her? Or was it better to go along quietly and wait for a better opportunity to happen?

If she did not hit Raoul, what were her other options? Midland was approximately four hours from Ciudad Juarez, the closest border crossing. Raoul probably had his family plane on the other side of the border—on this short notice, he probably hadn't been able to get clearance to land in America without arousing the suspicions of drug-enforcement officers.

Raoul might stop at a restroom before they crossed the border, especially if she threatened to relieve herself in the seat of his favorite car. She could try to slip away then. Or she could cause a scene at the border crossing. It might get her arrested and searched by the American customs officials, but it would keep her from getting on a plane with Raoul. Once he had her in Mexico, on his personal property, it would be much, *much* harder to get free of him.

What would her mother have done? She would have hit Raoul. She would not have waited for the just-right time. Mama would have been frantic to get back to her children, Gabriella realized. For so long, Gabriella had felt anger toward her mother for not going along—for not living to tell the tale. But now she understood. Fear had driven Mama to desperate measures.

Still, if she were going to hit Raoul, it would be better if he were not driving.

They were nearing the edge of Midland now. Billboards advertising fast-food restaurant were visible in the distance. But they were still far away from anything that resembled hustle or bustle, especially this early on a Saturday. She should wait until they were in a more populated area—safety in numbers and all that.

Unexpectedly a blue pickup pulled up alongside the

Porsche. *Odd,* Gabriella thought as the vehicle started honking, *that looks like Chance's truck.*

The truck shot forward and then came to a screeching halt some hundred feet in front of Raoul's car, blocking the road entirely.

"¿Qué carajo?" Raoul sputtered, swerving wildly.

Joaquin got out and began to walk toward the car, almost as if he wanted Raoul to run him down in the line of duty.

"¡Mierda!" Raoul cried, jerking the wheel so violently that Gabriella was sure the Porsche went up on two wheels. They spun in a tight circle before coming to a rest in the middle of the road.

When her head stopped spinning, she realized Raoul was trying to open the glove box. Of course—she should have realized he probably had a weapon with him. The moment he got it open, she slammed it shut on his fingers. He howled. Seconds later, the driver's door opened and Raoul was unceremoniously jerked out of the car.

Then her door opened and Chance was there. He held out a hand for her. "Are you okay, babe?"

"Take your hands off me, *idiota!*" Raoul shouted from the other side of the car.

"I got you," Chance said, his voice low and reassuring. "You can get out now. He can't touch you again."

She took his hand and was surprised to see that her arm was trembling. He helped her out of the car and pulled her into a strong embrace. Her whole body started to shake.

"I got you, babe," he said as he walked her away from the Porsche. "I got you."

"Chance," she managed to say, but her throat closed up, pushing her dangerously close to crying. And she would not let Raoul see her cry.

"She is mine!" Raoul yelled across the highway. *"¡Es mía!"*

"I'm taking her back where she belongs." Heavens, was that her brother? Had he been in the truck?

"She's coming to Mexico with me," Raoul all but snarled. "That is what Rodrigo and I agreed upon." He then made a little squeaking noise. Had Joaquin hit him? Or had Alex?

"Are you okay?" Chance asked again. His arms were still around her, his chest warm against hers. It was still early enough that there wasn't any other traffic on the road.

"Some bruises," she admitted, trying to block out the sounds of Raoul and Alex arguing about who had the right to take her to which home.

She didn't want anyone to take her. She just wanted to *go*.

Chance pushed her back so he could look at her. "I called Nathan. He'll arrest him for battery and attempted kidnapping."

She gasped as she got a good look at his face. "What happened?" she asked as she touched the massive black eye that covered half his face.

His smile was crooked, which made him wince. "Your brother punched me because I made you cry."

"¡Dios!" The tears tried to move up again, but the sounds of shouting reminded her that she couldn't fall apart, not yet.

"I want you to hear it from me," he went on, completely ignoring the argument behind him, "that there's nothing going on between me and Cara. She's got a problem and she needed a shoulder to cry on and some advice—nothing more. I would *never* step out on you."

She knew that, of course—but to hear him say it made her weak not with fear but with relief. "I know. I talked with her last night. We met at the diner. She explained her…problem to me." She grinned up at him. "What does 'step out' mean?"

His smile got wider. "Cheat, babe. I'd never cheat."

Behind them, the sound of the fight was getting louder. "What do you want to do?"

Part of her wanted him to sweep her off her feet and carry her away from all of this—Raoul, Joaquin, Alex. From her father, who'd arranged this "marriage."

"Because whatever you want," he said, his poor bruised face quite serious, "the answer is yes."

He was asking her. Not even Alex was asking what she wanted—he was still arguing with Raoul about who got to do what with her.

"If you want to go with this *cabrón*," Chance said, pronouncing the profanity in Spanish perfectly, "then I'll step aside. If you want to go back to Alex's house and stay with your father, that's fine, too."

"I do not want to do either of those things. I never want to see Raoul again."

That time, Chance did not wince through his grin. "Done." He turned. "Joaquin! See that Raoul leaves. Alone."

"Sí," Joaquin replied, shoving Raoul toward the Porsche.

"Wait—I think Raoul has a gun in the glove box." She could see him firing at all of them as he drove away, not caring who he hit.

One of Chance's eyebrows—the one over the unbruised eye—jumped up. "Check the glove box first," he yelled over his shoulder.

Gabriella watched in amazement as Joaquin did exactly what Chance asked of him. He shoved Raoul roughly at Alex, who caught the man and held him tight. The Joaquin went through the car, starting with the glove box. He pulled out the handgun but found nothing else.

Chance kept a strong arm around her shoulder, but he didn't try to shield her from the scene in front of them. It was then that she saw Alex's red Ferrari behind Raoul's car. Raoul was completely blocked in. For some reason, it made her happy that her brother had come with Chance, even if he was arguing that Gabriella should go back with him.

Chance turned back to her, that twinkle in his eyes. "Will you get in the truck so I can move it? I don't want to be in Raoul's way as he leaves."

She nodded and climbed up. Alex went back to his car to move it, as well, but Joaquin stood on the shoulder of the road, Raoul's gun aimed at the area where Raoul's knee probably was on the other side of the car door.

Chance slid into the driver's seat and moved the truck off to the side of the road. Raoul roared past them, making a variety of offensive hand gestures as he went.

Then it was quiet. Gabriella looked in the rearview mirror. Joaquin crossed the road, his eyes trained on Raoul's rapidly disappearing car.

"What happened?" Chance asked, reaching over—but not taking her hand. Waiting for him. Asking permission.

She didn't hesitate. She entwined her fingers with his. "Joaquin woke me up and hurried me downstairs. Before I knew it, I was in the car and Raoul was driving off. He said...he said my father called him because I wasn't safe in America anymore."

"Yeah, that's pretty much what he told me, too."

"Why is Joaquin taking orders from you? *He* betrayed me. *He* put me in the car with Raoul."

"Well, now—funny story." He ran his thumb over her knuckles. "I think ol' Joaquin felt lower than a rattler's belly in a wheel rut about that—and then your father up and fired him on the spot because the big man let you spend time with me. So I hired him—head of security on McDaniel's Acres. New position."

Gabriella shook her head, unsure if she could trust her ears. "You *hired* Joaquin?"

"He took the job. Told me what Raoul was driving, which way he'd gone."

Well. There was that. Joaquin felt remorse and had tried to redeem himself. Alex cared enough to help find her.

But Chance had come for her. She knew that neither her brother nor her bodyguard would have attempted this grand rescue without Chance pulling them both along.

"So now," Chance said, raising her hand to his lips and kissing it, "I think it's time for you to tell me what you want to happen next."

She looked around. A few cars had gone past them. Joaquin was still standing opposite Chance's truck, the gun nowhere in sight. Alex was in his car behind the truck.

"I want to do what I want. I want to come and go and not have to report in or be 'protected.' I want to ride and work metal and be happy. I want to be free."

Chance looked down at where their hands were joined. It was almost as if this pronouncement worried him. Then he said, "Hang on." He let go of her hand and opened his door. "Joaquin—you want to get a ride back with Alex? Come out to the ranch later. We'll start the paperwork."

Joaquin stared at the two of them for a moment before nodding his head and walking back to Alex's car. Carefully, her brother drove over the grassy median until he was pointed back toward Royal, Texas.

She waited until Alex's car was gone. Alone. They were finally, truly alone. Up to this point, Chance had been wonderful asking her what she wanted. But the truth was she wanted him. And she wanted to be sure that he wanted her, too. So she asked, "What about you?"

"I want to keep my land in McDaniels' hands. I want to come home to a good woman in my bed. I want to have some babies that learn to ride horses and jump into swimming holes." His voice was low. She looked at him. From this side, she couldn't see his bruised face at all. "I'd like to do all those things with you."

Yes. To share her bed with him, to be a mother—the things that had always seemed out of reach. "Will you have Joaquin follow me around? I don't want to be protected anymore, Chance."

"Nope. If you want to go for a ride or to town for coffee alone, that's fine by me. If you want Joaquin to drive you, that's okay, too. But if you want me to come with you," he said, looking her in the eye, "well, all you have to do is ask. You already know the answer."

Yes. The answer would be *yes.*

"I do not want to live in sin. I will attend church every Sunday."

The corner of his mouth crooked up in the way that spoke volumes about what kind of sin he might be able to live with. "I can have a preacher at the ranch tomorrow morning."

She tilted his face. The bruise was truly spectacular— one that would take some time to fade away. "Perhaps we should wait. Just a little bit."

But did that mean she would have to go back to Alex's house? Where her father would no doubt try to bend her to his will again?

Chance must have read her mind. "You know, I got this great big hotel—real nice place. Not too crowded right now. You can have any room you want, for as long as you want."

"And Joaquin?" She *so* wanted to be free—not just the illusion of freedom, but the real thing. And yet...the idea scared her, just a little. This must be how a caged animal felt when it was finally released back into the wild— freedom could be a little overwhelming.

"I got a room for him on the ground floor where he can

keep tabs on who's coming and going. Franny'll cook him dinner. I'm not worried about him."

Yes, she thought, that would be good. She did not know if she would ever see her father again. But Joaquin—he had always been more of a father to her, anyway. "I can set up my workshop?"

"We'll get your horse shipped up—all your things. Anything you want." He leaned over, cupping her chin in his hand and lifted her mouth to his. "Gabriella del Toro, will you marry me?"

She could not help herself. "You already know the answer, don't you, Chance McDaniel?"

"Yeah," he said, brushing his lips against hers. "I do."

* * * * *

TEXAS CATTLEMAN'S CLUB: THE MISSING
MOGUL
Don't miss a single story!

RUMOR HAS IT by Maureen Child
DEEP IN A TEXAN'S HEART by Sara Orwig
SOMETHING ABOUT THE BOSS... by Yvonne Lindsay
THE LONE STAR CINDERELLA by Maureen Child
TO TAME A COWBOY by Jules Bennett
IT HAPPENED ONE NIGHT by Kathie DeNosky
BENEATH THE STETSON by Janice Maynard
WHAT A RANCHER WANTS by Sarah M. Anderson
THE TEXAS RENEGADE RETURNS by Charlene Sands